ZACH TRAGIC IN
FORGOTTEN TOKYO

ZACH TRAGIC IN FORGOTTEN TOKYO

A NEAR-FUTURE BAD LUCK THRILLER

M. DAVID SCOBLE

M&W
Books
Baltimore · Tokyo

Moogi and Wil Books, LLC
Baltimore, Maryland
www.mandwbooks.com

Library of Congress Control Number: 2020914500

First Edition

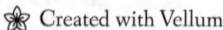 Created with Vellum

FREE STORIES FROM M&W BOOKS

Would you like to get more short stories for free? Join the *M&W Books Pack*! We send a newsletter with a free short story every month!

Click *M&W Books* to join the newsletter or scan the QR code below!

For Joy, Alexander, and Elysia.

For Moogi and Wil, as they journey on the other side of the Rainbow Bridge.
For Zachtaloctl and the Truffinator.

Most of all, for my father without whom I never would have travelled to Asia and learned what it means to live in a big city. Now I live in the biggest city.

PREFACE

Zach Tragic in Forgotten Tokyo is a set of stories based in Japanese language and folklore. Japanese notoriously borrows and reutilizes words from other languages, claiming the new words as the language's own. The characters in Zach Tragic's stories would normally speak Japanese, so to include the feel of incorporating of foreign words into Japanese, I have used Japanese words throughout the English language story.

Enjoy a small taste of the fusion of language that happens every day in the real and Forgotten Tokyo...

1

TRAGIC AND THE POISONER

RUFUS, THE LAWYER, AND THE ONIGIRI

"You are responsible for everything. Now you're gonna pay up, Tragic." Rufus said. Rufus wasn't his actual name, just what everyone in Toranomon Downs called the short thug. That was about the time his fist hit my nose. I was expecting it and took the punch. It still hurt like hell.

"Hold on there, Rufus. I brought you in to see Zach on an understanding." That was Saito, my lawyer. A good lawyer is necessary in any line of work in Forgotten Tokyo, but especially in my line of work.

"This gaikoku only understands one thing, my fists." Rufus was not the wittiest of local tough thugs. He was, however, very tough. I was not about to take another fist in the face. I caught Rufus' wrist and twisted it around. No mean feat when you are sitting in a cheap, used office chair and the guy hitting you is standing, yet still barely above eye-level. I pulled Rufus into his swing, my left hand carrying his left hook around in front of me. I pulled him up short and kicked out with my foot, tripping up his. Rufus went sprawling on the floor as my used office chair glided back on the old caster wheels. He landed with a loud smack, like landing belly first on a concrete floor.

"Mr. Lejeune, please, there is no need for violence." Saito said. I looked at him with my best high eyebrow, questioning look.

"Saito-san, I value your advice as a lawyer, but seriously? I'm hardly being violent. Aikido isn't a hard art." I said. I began to have my doubts about my lawyer's counsel.

"Ow, what hit me?" Rufus moaned on my floor.

"The concrete floor hit you. Probably on your belly, since that seems to be where you're laid out." I said to the thug on my floor, "I hope you aren't bleeding in here, my cleaner is not fond of bloodstains."

"Mr. Lejeune," My lawyer said as he placed his briefcase on my desk. It was a quality case, real leather, not one of the synthetic ones that were popular these days. Almost everything in Forgotten Tokyo was a synthetic, except for the food and the people.

"Saito-san, why did you bring this fellow here? I know he hired us for the brothel job, but that was resolved." I asked, standing and walking over to my open window. The other escape option was the door, but it was unfortunately closed. Quicker to just out the window and down the fire escape ladder. Just like the brothel job.

"That's it, Mr. Lejeune. Mr. Nakajima is unsatisfied with the work and would like a refund. I explained that we do not provide refunds and that he agreed to our terms when he hired you for the inspection of the facility." Saito was explaining, but I wasn't really interested. Rufus stood up and appeared to be gathering his wits, such as they were. I looked out the window as a breeze blew in. The air was hot. Everything in July is hot in the city. The wind, the water, the tempers. The breeze blew some papers off my desk and onto the floor between me and Rufus. Well then, if that is how it was going to be, I guess the window might be an option after all.

"You son-of-a-bitch, Tragic. I paid you to protect my building, not burn it down." Rufus was gathering his strength to start the fight again.

"You paid me to find the problems. I found the problems. You chose to store all that old paper in your brothel. It was a fire trap. It wasn't my fault that your fire trap did what fire traps do." I spoke quietly. Sometimes people listen when you speak quietly.

"That was all my kompromat. Where the hell else would I store it?" Rufus yelled. Kompromat. The old Soviet term. Compromising information. Great. Bribery materials. I didn't know the brothel was a front at the time, but I did suspect it. Now I knew why Rufus was upset. The fire cost him millions. Perhaps more. Toranomon Downs was the go to place for government malfeasance. The days of being a respectable business district were far in the past.

"I am going to take my losses out of your hide, troubleshooter." Rufus bellowed and charged at me. I braced for what I knew was coming.

It was anti-climactic.

Rufus took one step, and his foot landed on the papers that fell off my desk. His shoes were well worn; the synthetic leather soles were glass smooth. He slipped. Rufus wasn't fat, but he wasn't a small man either. This time he hit the concrete floor flat on his back.

"Don't get up, Rufus. It isn't safe." I said.

"That a threat, Tragic? You think this hurts me?" Rufus moaned from the floor. Tough talk, but he didn't get up.

"Saito-san, can you get the door for Nakajima-san? I think we are done here." I instructed the counselor.

"Sure, Mr. Lejeune."

I extended my hand to Rufus. It wasn't his fault. He didn't know. If anything, it was my fault. It's always my fault. Rufus took my hand, and I pulled him up.

"Look, Rufus, Nakajima-san, I'm sorry about the brothel. I don't care about your kompromat, but I am sorry about the building and your livelihood. But you came to me. You know why people come to me."

"I know, Zach, but my employees, they rely on me to provide for them. I'm out of business. The bengoshi said we could find a compromise." Rufus was more reasonable. Concrete floors have a way of helping people see reason.

"I know they do. You are not a bad boss, just unlucky." I was being overly nice. Some egos need a massage, "But you can't come into my office and blame me for your misfortune. I told you about the fire hazard. I told you about the wiring problems. You chose to install that ridiculous VR system."

"Zach, the money was too good. The bengoshi said it was worth it," Rufus was rambling. Who ever his lawyer was, he was a bad one. Probably a half-wit or worse, a rental.

"Look, Rufus, I saved the important part of your establishment. The people. The building burned, we all escaped out the windows. Rebuild. Go into something less risky. Here, have a rice ball, think about your options, okay?" I pointed at my lawyer and the mini-fridge. He got the hint and grabbed an onigiri from the box for Rufus.

"Thanks. Zach, sorry. I just get so mad. It's the easiest way to deal with things down here, you know?" Rufus said. He probably got a good knock on the head when he slipped on the paper.

The lawyer handed him the onigiri. Onigiri makes everything better.

"Thanks, counselor. Thanks." Rufus took the rice ball wrapped in cellophane and I saw him to the door.

The hot air hit us as we stepped out onto the platform. The entry to the office was in an open space in the building. The natural breeze was cold in winter and hot in summer. The stairs down were better than the elevator and Rufus took them slowly as he left.

The opposite door opened as I watched Rufus leave. Fukusawa poked her head out. Erika was a snoop. Everything that happened in our old building was her business. She was also the landlord.

"Zach-chan, another satisfied customer?" Fukusawa asked. The fight was loud, and Erika wasn't a naïf.

"Erika-sama, just a minor discussion about lawyers." I said.

Saito frowned.

"You know how I feel about the bengoshi, Zach-chan. Worst way to make a living. I tolerate yours because of how good you are to me." Fukusawa winked at me and laughed. She closed her door. Saito and I did the same. Once the door was closed, I looked Saito up and down.

"Tell me again why I retain your services?"

"Mr. Lejeune, please. How was I to know Rufus would get violent?" Saito looked pained, as if merely questioning his competence was an assault.

"Saito, you know half my clients are unstable and the other half blame me for their failures. I expect you to keep the two separate from each other. When someone is both unstable and blames me for their problems, I need you to keep them far away." I explained to my lawyer.

"But you can take care of yourself, Zach." Saito was relaxing.

"Not about me, Saito-san, it is for their own good. You

saw the breeze. The paper. Rufus could have hit his head and gotten a concussion. Or worse. Remember the fire." I was about to explain my talent to Saito again when there was a knock on the office door.

"What is it, Rufus? Do you want another onigiri?" I called out. The door opened. It wasn't Rufus.

"Mr. Lejeune? I'm Kato, with the police. There is a dead body outside. Can you come with me?"

THE BODY, THE DETECTIVE, AND THE FUGU

"A dead body? Why does this concern me?" I asked, staring at the uniformed officer in the doorway, "Kato-san, was it?"

"Yes, Lejuene-sama, Officer Kato. Please come with me?" Kato said without further explanation.

"Naruhodo." I said, "Saito-san, can you come with me? It seems I may need my lawyer."

"I'll get my case and be right there." Saito said, looking through the papers on my desk.

I followed Officer Kato out. He was a new, young officer. I hadn't seen him around the area before. Police in Forgotten Tokyo rotate between kobans, the little miniature police stations spread throughout the city. Many things really hadn't changed from before the Drift and police routines were one of those things. Every few weeks a new set of officers rotated to the koban, and you had to break the new guys in all over again.

"Over here, please." Kato led me over to the balcony next to the stairs down. He looked towards the edge. I took the hint and leaned over, looking down to the street. Rufus.

"You are correct, Officer Kato. There is a dead body down there. I still don't see how this concerns me." I feigned disinterest.

"The Detective Inspector will be along soon. Please wait here, Lejuene-sama." Kato made no move to leave. Wait with him. So I don't run. Kato was ready to pronounce me guilty, that much was obvious.

My lawyer trundled up beside me. He leaned over the balcony edge a little too far for my comfort and whistled. Saito righted himself and looked at me and then at Kato.

"Well, so much for Nakajima-san. I guess we don't have to worry about him anymore." My idiot lawyer said to Kato and me.

"Seriously, why did I hire you, Saito? Where did you go to school, even?" It disgusted me. I would have been better off with a rental bengoshi.

"Well, I guess that establishes that you know the victim." The bloated voice came from behind me. I turned, and a man in business casual was working his way up the steps. The short sleeve dress shirt was already slick with a layer of sweat. The man clearly didn't get out in the weather on a daily basis.

"And you are?" I asked.

"Detective Inspector Jones." Kato said, snapping to attention.

"Relax, Kato." The man said, "I am Detective Inspector Jones. I presume you are Mr. Lejeune? Zachary Lejeune? Pleased to meet you."

The sweaty detective offered his meishi in one hand. Despite the insult, I took the business card in both hands and examined it. The kanji read Watanabe Ichiro, not Jones. I flipped to the back and saw it had English text. The English side read Watanabe 'Jones' Ichiro, Chief

Detective Inspector. I reached into my vest pocket for my card holder.

"You are correct, I am Lejeune. Zach Lejeune. Just Zach, not Zachary." I flicked out my meishi and proffered it to CDI 'Jones' in the proper fashion. Jones took it with one hand, stubby thumb and fingers bending the card stock as he snatched it from me.

"I don't stand on formality, Lejeune." Jones said, flipping my card around to read both sides. Disappointed, CDI Jones jammed the meishi into his shirt pocket. I heard my lawyer cluck his tongue while I merely frowned.

"Naruhodo. What can I do for you, CDI Jones?" I said as I placed his meishi into my card holder.

"Admission of guilt would be nice. Can we start with that, or do you want to do the whole folk dance routine?" Jones said. Kato kept his mouth shut. My lawyer clucked.

"Folk dance routine?" I asked.

"Something we say in the countryside. I'm seconded from Yamanashi." Jones replied.

"Naruhodo."

"I am Mr. Lejeune's lawyer," Saito said, using the English version of -san.

"Folk dance it is. Kato, go down there and make sure they do the mobile forensic tests properly. That was your best subject at the academy, wasn't it?" Jones said to the uniformed Officer Kato.

"Yes, sir. Understood." Kato said and swiftly left down the stairs.

"Kids. Now, do we really need your lawyer, Lejeune?"

"CDI Jones. Watanabe-san. I always conduct business with my lawyer present." I said, stepping away from the sweaty policeman.

"Jones. No one calls me Watanabe." He was an older

man. Slightly balding. Clearly a career detective, but from the prefectures, not the National Police. The connection between Forgotten Tokyo and the rest of the country had fractured after the Drift, but not so badly that talented professionals from the countryside didn't make their way into the city. I wasn't sure if CDI Jones was a talented professional or just a thorn in the Yamanashi police Director-General's backside.

"Naruhodo." I said. Disappointed.

"So. You know the victim. Rufus, did I hear your lawyer say his name was? Is he a gaikoku or half?" CDI Jones was undeterred.

"He was Japanese. Nakajima Amaro was his name. He was a client of mine." I said, looking at my lawyer and willing the counselor to keep his mouth shut and let the professionals deal with things.

"I see. What exactly did this Nakajima-san hire you to do, Mr. Lejeune? What is your business, exactly?" CDI Jones poked my vest with his finger. Wonderful.

"I am a troubleshooter. I find problems and report them to my clients." I said.

"And what sort of problems did you find for the unfortunate Nakajima-san?" Jones asked. He rested his finger on my vest and stepped a half-shuffle closer. I noticed the move. He practiced kendo. He was good, too. My lawyer never even noticed the way Jones stepped. I looked up from CDI Jones' fat, sweaty finger.

"Fire hazard." I said, taking a half step back and to my left. Jones recognized the move. He sized me up, kendo-ka to kendo-ka.

Jones dropped his finger. Detente.

"Uhn. I see. Was Nakajima-san as pleased with your conclusions?" CDI Jones turned away and looked out over the street. A few meters away were the buildings on the other side of our small road. The road didn't really have a name, it was just the 1st intersection, 3rd road.

"With the conclusions? No problem. The results well, Nakajima-san didn't follow our advice." I said. Let the CDI earn his pay.

"And?"

"The brothel he ran burned to the ground."

"And he came here to express his displeasure, I assume?" CDI Jones said.

"Of course. Nakajima-san was concerned for his business, for his employees. I gave him some advice. Find a new line of business." I said. No sense in trying to deceive CDI Jones. My idiot lawyer probably would have told the entire story, anyway.

"I see." said Jones.

"Naruhodo."

"CDI Jones," Kato called from the street, "We have the results from the portable forensic lab."

"I'll be right down," Jones shouted at Kato, "You'll stay here, Mr. Lejeune."

"Naruhodo."

CDI Jones tromped back down the stairs to the street level. I looked over the balcony and watched as he walked up to Officer Kato. The two stood over the body of Amaro 'Rufus' Nakajima.

Kato showed a paper printout to CDI Jones, pointed to a few lines of text, then at Rufus. CDI Jones just nodded.

"I don't like this, Zach." said Saito.

"Neither do I, counselor, neither do I."

Kato pointed at another line of text. Jones leaned in, then pointed at the half-eaten onigiri still clutched in Rufus' hand.

"I think I need a reference, Saito. You know any criminal defenders?" I asked as CDI Jones looked up and directly at me. He might have been good at kendo, but Jones did not have a poker face at all.

"I can find someone for you, why?"

"I think CDI Jones is about to arrest me for murdering Rufus." I said.

"What? How can you even think that?" Saito asked.

CDI Jones bounded up the stairs, no sign of his previous, sweaty struggle to the second floor. He stepped up to me sharply as I turned to face him. I expected to be arrested, I didn't expect to be assaulted. CDI Jones grabbed my vest with both hands and yanked me down into his face.

"You poison that son-of-a-bitch, Lejeune? What kind of man poisons his own client? Tetrodotoxin in the fish? Slipped Nakajima a fugu liver, did you, Lejeune?" Jones was mad. He mixed English into his Japanese and I could barely understand him.

"CDI Jones, please, my client."

"Shut up, Saito." Jones and I said at the same time. I cracked a smile.

"I don't poison my clients, Chief Detective Inspector. Now how about you stop ruining my clothes with your filthy paws?" I said, sweetly. Jones let go of my vest, leaving sweaty hand prints behind on the fabric.

"Fine. You are under arrest on suspicion of murder." Jones said, taking a step back and turning away from me, "You son-of-a-bitch."

I didn't expect Jones to move as fast as he did. He pivoted and landed a right jab directly on my nose. I am not ashamed to say I went down like a falling rock.

THE KOBAN, THE QUESTIONS, AND THE BENTOS

I woke in the koban. I was in the cooling cell, and it was anything but cool. The cells in the koban in front of the abandoned American Embassy were on the second floor. There was air conditioning, but only enough so the drunks didn't die of dehydration or heat sweats in the night. The local police kept power usage at a minimum, so I was covered in a light sweat.

I cracked my jaw as I sat up. The police can get away with many things, but I wasn't ready to let this slide. CDI Jones wouldn't get the drop on me again.

I waited a good half-hour. I would have checked my watch, but it and all my personal possessions were gone. I had a clear plastic folder with a variety of receipts and assorted bureaucratic sundries contained within. I glanced over the receipts, confirming they documented all my belongings. They were.

The door opened. The cooling cells were little more than rooms with a bench that doubled as a bed. There were no bars. That was a fiction of the old television dramas and movies. Kato stood in the open doorway.

"CDI Jones will see you now." Kato said. I raised an eyebrow at him.

"Certainly." I said, "Wouldn't want to keep the detective waiting."

Kato took me out and into the narrow hallway. I was in the farthest cell from the stairs down. The interview room was the last door before the stairs.

"You know the way?" Kato asked.

"The koban isn't that big, Kato." I was not amused, even if Kato was new to the area. I walked the seven steps to the interview room door.

"Come in, Lejeune." CDI Jones said from inside. I opened the door and stepped into the tiny room. The interview room was just a converted cell. Two chairs and a fold out desk instead of an uncomfortable bench for sleeping.

"Well, you look at home, detective." I said.

"Are you a funny guy, Lejeune? Because that almost sounded funny. Wasn't that funny, Officer Kato?" Jones started with banter. Familiar, but aggressive.

"Yes sir, hilarious, CDI Jones." Kato spoke as expected. I didn't think he liked his CDI.

"Lejeune, sit." I sat where Jones pointed. The chair was older than my office chair and far less clean.

"Where's my lawyer, Jones?" I decided I would not play the game.

"Saito? Haven't seen him. Maybe he gave up on you? Kato close the door behind you."

"I wouldn't be that lucky." I said.

"And why is that, Mr. Lejeune? Is it because of your reputation? The way I hear it, bad things happen when you are around. Real bad things. You a fire bug, Lejeune? Did Rufus find out you set that fire in his place? Did he come for revenge?" CDI Jones was testing the waters. He must have read something about me from his predecessor and assumed he knew me. CDI Jones didn't know me.

"CDI Jones, let me help you out. It's true that bad things happen around me. All the time. We live in bad times. Bad things happen, but they don't need me to make them happen." I tried to tell Jones the quick version of my talent, the version for people who don't believe in luck.

"Oh, I see. So you just happen to be there when the fire breaks out in the brothel. You just happen to be there when an assembly line suffers a critical failure and grinds to a halt. You just happen to be found right at the center of the subsidence that destroyed the entire metro station at Kanda during the 3rd Great Kanto Earthquake. Untouched. That all seems a little coincidental to me, Mr. Lejeune." Jones flipped through a pile of papers, counting off my near misses as he read the title lines on each report.

"Yes. I did. And I wasn't unharmed. I think if you bothered reading more than just the summaries, you would know that."

"Why do they call you Zach Tragic?" CDI Jones was just getting wound up.

"Please, don't call me that." I said.

"What? Zach Tragic? The guy they hire to find things and make them go wrong? Zach Tragic, the troubleshooter? The guy who has a love affair with disasters? Why shouldn't I call you that? Your history is littered with reports of destruction, catastrophe, and loss." Jones was yelling. He seemed to take my relationship with bad luck personally.

"My name, CDI Jones, is Zach Lejeune."

"Tragedy follows you!" CDI Jones beat his fist against the reports on the desk. His anger didn't feel like an act. It had to be, but it sure didn't feel like it.

"Lunch." Kato knocked and opened the door.

"Kato, not now. I am interrogating the prisoner."

"CDI Jones, Tragic's lawyer is here as well." Kato definitely didn't like Jones. He was smiling.

"Fine. Get out. You stay here, Tragic. I'll send your lawyer up." CDI Jones pushed past me and slammed the door closed behind him.

I heard the detective tromp down the stairs. Even his footsteps were angry. Smaller steps got louder. Saito was coming up the steps. The door opened, and my lawyer with his leather brief entered.

"Have a seat, Saito-san. You find a criminal defender for me?" I asked as my lawyer sat in CDI Jones' chair.

"Zach, it's bad." Saito opened his brief and pulled out a thick folder.

"I know it's bad. That new detective from the countryside cold-cocked me and threw me in a cell. Of course it's bad. What about a criminal lawyer?" I said, frustrated with Saito. At one time, I thought he was competent counsel. Now I nursed serious doubts.

"Look at this, they've built a solid case against you. It isn't just Rufus, either. The Oita factory incident is here. So is the Kanda problem." Saito tossed the thick folder at me. Some grains of cooked rice fell off the folder. Apparently, lunch had started early.

"So? The Tokyo Police know all about me. Hell, I work for them often enough, they know I just attract misfortune. I don't cause these things to happen. And Kanda? Are they seriously thinking of blaming an earthquake on me?" I looked at the folder and turned the pages. It seemed like each page smelled like salt. Lunch must have been aji, or some other ocean fish.

"Zach. You can't expect everyone to believe you are

some sort of supernatural bad luck charm." Saito said, reviving our old argument.

"Saito-san, please. You know if something bad can happen, it happens when I am around. It isn't supernatural, it isn't magic. I'm just a magnet for bad luck. Murphy's law, like they say out west. I am the special corollary. Anything that can go wrong, will go wrong, especially when Zach Tragic is around." I said as I closed the folder. I was angry, and I could feel my fingers tingling.

I heard a loud crash from inside the koban. Something had fallen on the first floor. Another crash followed. Heavy, labored steps made their way up to the second floor. Saito got up, he was agitated.

"Something wrong, Saito-san?" I asked, looking at my lawyer. The room seemed to get warmer.

"Didn't you hear that? Something's wrong." Saito said as he opened the door.

"Yeah, I can tell something is wrong. But it isn't because of me, is it, Saito-san?" I said, calm like oil. The vents had stopped pushing cool air in.

"Rufus wasn't enough, was he, Tragic? You had to have a body count, didn't you?" CDI Jones said from the hallway. His voice was loud, but there was a weakness to it. Vulnerability and perhaps fear. I heard the hammer on a revolver cock. The police in Forgotten Tokyo still used revolvers, at least they still carried them.

"Now, now. We can't have you shooting anyone, Detective Inspector." Saito said from the hallway. I listened for the compressors, but the air conditioner was definitely cut off.

"Chief Detective Inspector, you bengoshi scum." CDI Jones cried out in pain. I heard a bone crack.

"Thank you for this lovely weapon, CDI Jones. I am

sure it will come in useful." Saito came back into the inter-view room, closing the door behind him. He sat and pointed the cocked revolver at my chest. His hand rested on his leather brief.

"You don't seem surprised, Zach. You can't have me believe you knew this was coming?" Saito said smoothly. Sweat beaded on my lawyer's forehead.

"I didn't. Not until you gave me the reports." I said honestly.

"Oh? Well, do tell *Mr. Lejeune*, what did the reports tell you?" Saito was smug. It wasn't a pleasant look on him.

"It was the rice. Well, honestly, the rice and the oil." I said, flicking a single white grain at my lawyer.

"Oh? You knew something was up because of rice and oil?" Saito asked. My lawyer took a handkerchief from his pocket and wiped his brow.

"Well, at first I thought it was just lunch. You carry your brief everywhere. You must have had your lunch early and spilled some rice on the folder the police gave you. Then my fingers tingled." I said.

"And you knew from that? Maybe you are just inca-pable of emotion. There is no way you saw this betrayal coming." Saito didn't believe me.

"The tetrodotoxin. It was in the onigiri. It was also on the folder. That is why my fingers tingled. You probably laced it in the bentos for the police while you waited to see me." I said, "You had to have it in your brief when you brought Rufus up to see me. Gave him a poisoned onigiri."

"Well, you are clever." Saito said.

"What I don't understand is why. Why kill Rufus?" I asked, playing for time. I knew the signs when Murphy was paying me a visit.

"I didn't want to kill Rufus. The onigiri was for you." Saito wiped himself again, sweat beading on his face.

"And an opportunity presented itself? Is that why Rufus had to die?" I asked.

"Yes, dammit. So I could get back at you. So you would finally get your comeuppance." Saito said as he pulled the trigger.

THE LAWYER, THE BULLET, AND THE KOBAN

THE HEAT WAS UNBEARABLE. FORGOTTEN TOKYO IN summer is a terrible place to live. Saito was from Akita. He moved to Forgotten Tokyo a couple years earlier and still suffered in the summer months. The sweat was getting in his eyes and causing him to shake.

I watched Saito blink away the salty sweat. He wiped with his handkerchief and let his grip slacken. The beloved leather brief was a soft leather, terrible for bracing his gun hand. When Saito's eyes stopped blinking away the sweat, and he firmed up his shoulders, I knew it was time to act. I kicked away the leg of the fold out desk.

When Saito pulled the trigger, the table was already falling and his brief, hand, and the revolver falling with it. The revolver had been cocked, so the trigger pull was light and I couldn't count on my talent to save me. Never count on luck. Good, bad, or tragic.

The gun fired. The bullet flew and hit my chair, right in the seat in front of me and between my legs. I felt the heat and the splinters from the wood of the chair strike my slacks. Saito would regret it if he ripped my one nice pair of slacks. Quality tailored goods were scarce these days.

"You idiot." Saito yelled. I didn't say a word. Instead, I punched my lawyer in the throat. It wasn't a tsuki strike, but it was close enough. Saito crumpled, but he still held the gun. I ran. Out the door, CDI Jones was sprawled on the top steps. I grabbed him and checked his face. He was alive. His hand was crushed, Saito must have stepped on it and ground the bones into the metal of the floor. I couldn't leave the detective there, Saito could finish him effortlessly.

I lifted Jones; he wasn't as heavy as he looked. Lucky me. I pulled him over my shoulder and started a buddy carry down the steps of the koban. I could hear Saito's hacking coughs clearing up. I should have hit him harder.

I was at the bottom step with Jones when I heard Saito moving above. The shot rang out and hit the wall next to me. Saito was a bad shot, but that wasn't anything to rely upon.

"Can you hear me, Jones? My lawyer has a gun. We need to get out of here." I said to the man I was carrying. He said something, but I couldn't understand his slurs.

The exit to the koban was only a few meters away. Kobans are small, glorified shacks. The old Beikoku koban was bigger, but still not over four or five meters in total length. Unburdened, I could make it out before Saito was down the stairs. I wasn't unburdened, and Kato and two other officers in the koban were laying across the route to the door. I was right, Saito had spiked the bentos with tetrodotoxin. I was trapped in a cop shop with a bunch of paralyzed uniforms and a drooling Chief Detective Inspector. My lawyer had a gun and wanted me dead. I had no idea why. Just my luck.

"Leave me. Get out, Tragic." Jones slurred.

"Don't call me Tragic."

"Zach. I'm coming to get you, you bastard." Saito laughed behind me. He was nuts, no two ways about it.

I put Jones down in a chair. Kato had fallen out of it when the tetrodotoxin had taken effect. I had to get to the door, lure Saito away from the helpless uniforms and CDI Jones.

I jumped over Kato and made it to the sliding glass door when I heard the hammer cocking behind me. I froze. No sense in dying on the run. I turned to face my lawyer.

"Counselor." I said.

"Mr. Lejeune." Saito said, aiming down the barrel of the revolver. The hammer was halfway back, the cylinder rotated midway. I could see the lead of the next bullet protruding from the weapon. I smiled.

"So, before you shoot me dead, care to tell me what this is all about, Saito-san?" I asked. I needed to buy some time.

"Not really. I hate making speeches."

"A lawyer that doesn't enjoy talking?" I cocked my eyebrow at Saito. He leered back at me.

"Let's just say the money was right. You've made enemies, Zach Tragic." Saito said.

"It's my lawyer's job to keep enemies away, or did you forget that, Saito-san?" I needed to seriously interrogate my hiring standards.

"I hate being your lawyer." Saito shouted at me.

"Fine. Your fired. Collect your remaining retainer and get out. Happy?" I kept my eyes on Saito. I didn't want him to look anywhere but at me.

"It's not that easy, Tragic."

"Stop calling me Tragic."

"Oh, you don't like that? Reminder that you are a bad luck charm? Murphy's corollary? Do you prefer Taira no

Masakado?" Saito pulled the hammer back, something locked, and he looked at the gun in his hand.

"You know nothing. He and I have nothing in common." I said. I didn't want Saito to see the bulging lead that blocked the cylinder from locking home. Bullets in Forgotten Tokyo were rare. Police used reloaded ammunition all the time and someone must not have crimped this particular bullet enough. The lead rode forward in the cartridge and blocked the action of the revolver. If something bad can happen, it will, especially around me.

"You were at Taira no Masakado's shrine. Stealing from a kami during the greatest disaster in the history of mankind. The Drift. The 3rd Great Kanto Earthquake. It was all because of you." Saito was mad in the eyes. He was almost right, but that really didn't count for anything.

"Saito-san. Counselor. Please, let's discuss things rationally." I had to get control of the situation. A lawyer with a gun is a terrible idea. An insane lawyer with a gun and a grudge is a recipe for disaster.

"No. No talking!" Saito couldn't make the revolver work, so he threw the weapon at me. He should have known better. Bad things happen around me. I am banned from every pachinko hall in Forgotten Tokyo. Seventeen restaurants refuse me service for fear of food poisoning. Eight companies ban me from their grounds. Five government officials insist I inspect those same companies regularly.

But Saito should have known better. Bad things don't happen out of the blue. Bad things happen because the potential was already present. I am just the catalyst. Ever since Kanda.

The gun hit the wall next to my head, fell to the ground and bounced. Then it went off. The bullet struck Saito, and he went down fast. I didn't have to do anything,

Saito made all the choices. The potential for an accident was always there. Accidents just happen when I am around.

"Help me." Saito said. I could barely hear him.

"Crap." I ran to his side, jumping over Kato again. Kato stirred. Good, I didn't need any dead uniforms on my conscience.

The bullet had struck Saito in the head, but it wasn't a clean hit. It looked like it hit the side of his cheek and maybe fractured the bones around his eye. Saito was a mess.

"Why Saito-san? You should have known better." I said, looking at my former lawyer with some pity and a touch of disgust.

"It was the money."

"Tragic, call 1-1-9." Jones croaked from his chair. I picked up the phone on the desk, punched the buttons for 1-1-9. Told them to send an ambulance. Then I told them to send three.

When the emergency vehicles arrived, everything was quiet. Saito wasn't dead, but he wasn't really doing a lot of talking. For all his bad luck, the good luck was the bullet glanced off his zygomatic bone and just broke most of the right side of his face. The doctors might even save the eye. Or not.

Jones was recovering. He didn't eat any of the bentos that Saito had tainted. Jones was just allergic to fugu. Being in the enclosed room with so much tetrodotoxin derived from the fugu liver had sent him into an allergic reaction. The paramedics treated him outside the koban and he was feeling like his sweaty, rude self in about an hour. They took Kato and the other uniformed officers to the hospital for observation and treatment. The air conditioning had failed and none of the police had really eaten very much of their bentos. The attempted poisoning ended up being mild overall.

"Tragic, get your lousy self out here." Jones was feeling better. I had finished making my statement to the relief officers and was just waiting for Jones to get himself together. I left the koban to talk to Jones.

"What can I do for you, CDI Jones?"

"Tragic. Get out of my koban and never come back." CDI Jones was sitting in a folding chair with a cooling patch pasted across his forehead.

"If you say so. Am I not under arrest anymore?" I smiled.

"Get out of my koban. I don't want to see you in a cell ever again."

"If you say so, CDI Jones." I smiled more.

"And Lejeune-sama, don't call me Jones. It's CDI Watanabe to you." The detective smiled as I walked away from his koban.

2

TRAGIC AND THE LAWYERS

THE NIGHT, THE LAWYERS, AND THE POLICE

"Zach-chan, you better not be sleeping in that office." Someone was pounding on my door. It felt uncomfortably like a hangover.

"Zach, you hear me?" Fukusawa. She owned the building, "If you sleep in there, I'll double your rent. It's an office, not a residence."

I'd been caught out. Again. Office space was cheap in Forgotten Tokyo. Living space was where the real money was at. Fukusawa wasn't interested in either the money or the problems that come with a residential permit.

"I'm here. Not sleeping." I called from the thin, roll out pad I used when I slept in the office.

"Well, good. You have some visitors. Not clients. They look like lawyers and I don't like them." Erika Fukusawa disliked most lawyers.

"Fine. Send them up." I was presentable enough for the bengoshi. My door opened, and three suits with occupants entered. Lawyers never seemed to have problems with fashion.

"How can I help you?" I said, looking from one suit to the next.

"Zach Lejeune?" The first lawyer asked. She was sharp with creased pleats and a razor-like set of lapels that dripped tears where they cut through my hangover.

"Depends on who you ask, but yeah, I'm Lejeune." I said, trying to avoid a cliché.

"Mr. Lejeune. We represent the government in the execution of the last will and testament of Nakajima Amaro." said the second occupant of a Savile Row suit, well worn. Probably a bengoshi hand-me-down. Family of lawyers, not the best, but probably full up on both money and debt.

"Naruhodo. What does this have to do with me?" I asked, interested. Rufus had died a month before, right outside my office building. My lawyer killed him and tried to frame and then murder me. It didn't take.

"Mr. Lejeune, you had a lien on Nakajima-san's business." The first razor-suit replied. The third suit, an OL special, handed me a document in a beige government envelope. She was the junior lawyer. The new suit was proof enough. Office Ladies and Salarymen always had the cheap, black suits. It was all they could afford.

"Naruhodo." I said, playing it safe. Never talk to a lawyer unless you have a lawyer. Then, don't talk to either of them.

"The lien, is significant." Savile Row said. A red sunburn peeked out from under his French cuffs.

"Naruhodo." I said.

I opened the envelope and took out the documents. The lien was significant. And incorrect.

"This is wrong." I said. Mistake number one. Never

contradict a lawyer, especially one in a suit that screams self-importance. The OL special winced.

"I assure you, Mr. Lejeune, it is correct. Your lawyer, Saito-sama placed the lien himself." Razor-suit said.

"I understand he is no longer with the legal bar?" Savile Row. A status hound, no doubt. Probably just returned from a vacation in the islands.

"Mr. Saito is indisposed at the moment. I did not hold a lien on Rufus' property. I forgave his debt." I said. The hangover was leading me into making more mistakes. Never talk to a lawyer in a fashionable suit.

"Well, Saito-sama was acting on the lien. On your behalf. Now, with Nakajima-san, sorry, Rufus as you know him, not having any heirs, I am sure you can see where this is going?" Razor-suit was enjoying this. I was positive they had a bet to decide who would be the main speaker.

"Naruhodo." I said.

"You are now the proud owner of Rufus' virtual experience business. Congratulation, you are the legal owner of a skinless brothel." Razor-suit smiled and turned on her ancient Juan Baptiste shoes and left. She practiced the move in front of a mirror at least of dozen times. Of that, I was sure.

Savile Row cleared his throat and pinched at his cufflinks. His arms were still raw from the exposure.

"Good day. Please remember to register your new occupation with the government, Mr. Lejeune."

OL special bowed. She nervously handed me her meishi, and I took it.

"Delighted." I said, looking at the card. Konno Asuka, it said. She bowed again and set down two more meishi. The cards of razor-suit and Savile Row.

"Hajimemashita. So sorry." Konno-san apologized and left after her sempai.

"Well. I guess I'm in a pile of steaming crap." I said to myself out loud. Maybe I should have stayed out in Tora-nomon Downs longer last night. My hangover cleared with the sudden acquisition of a questionable business. Fuku-sawa-san stood in my doorway.

"How long were you there?" I asked my landlady.

"The whole time. Skinless brothel, eh? One of those virtual arcades? You are in deep, Zach-chan." Fukusawa laughed, "Guess you get to use them for free now, right?"

"You know I don't do virtual. Things like that break when I'm around." I opened my desk drawer and pulled out a bottle and two glasses.

"Oh, celebrating?" she said from the doorway.

"Come on in, I think I need a drink and you can't drink umeshu alone." I said. Fukusawa walked over to my desk and pulled up a chair. She was the steady type, mid-forties to mid-fifties, tough. Survived everything and came out on top, or at least not in debt. Fukusawa owned my building and looked after everyone in it. Rumor had it she was a soldier once. Had an artificial arm to prove it. I figured she lost it in the 3rd Great Kanto Earthquake, but who knows. Knowing my luck, Fukusawa was a special operations veteran with a plasma rifle instead of a prosthetic limb. Or maybe just a cat lady. Who the hell knew, anymore?

"Zach-chan. I like you, but seriously. Unload this brothel. That is no way to make a living." Fukusawa poured the homemade umeshu from the bottle into our glasses.

"Naruhodo." I said.

"Listen son, don't feed me that line like you do everyone else. I know you. I gave you a place to stay after Kanda. You don't fool me." Her eyes twinkled. Damn, that got me. I could believe anything Fukusawa told me when she laid on the charm. Lucky for me I have a terminal case of disappointment.

"I know it. Even a legit skinless operation is trouble. Maybe the employees will buy it? Make it a common property?" I said, more hopeful than certain.

"Good luck with that, those sysadmins are probably in hock to old Rufus. If they could afford the business, they wouldn't be working there." My landlady was right. No one works in computers if they can afford it these days. The Drift made everything electronic a questionable profession. We downed the booze. Homemade umeshu is the best because you can make it as sweet or as bitter as you like. Mine is tart and sweet, a delicate balance.

Three glasses later and five laughs over my new status as a multiple small business owner, there was a second knock on my door.

"Closed for the day." I yelled.

"Lejeune-sama, please open up. It's Kato." The voice said.

Kato-san. Officer Kato from the local koban. A cop. Well, wasn't that just perfect?

"Come on in, Kato-san. I'll get you a glass, if you're off duty." I said.

Kato entered. He was one of the new crew of uniforms at the Akasaka koban. Fresh and green. He was still on duty. I put the glass down on my desk anyway, and Fukusawa poured a nice portion for Officer Kato.

"Lejeune-sama, Fukusawa-sama. Good morning. There has been an incident. I need you to accompany me to the coffee shop by the koban." Officer Kato was circumspect.

"Naruhodo. The coffee shop? Is that so?" I said rhetorically. Chief Detective Inspector 'Jones' Watanabe had banned me from the koban after my lawyer tried to poison all the police in it and shoot me dead with Jones' gun. It didn't take.

"There's been a death in Toranomon Downs. Witnesses say they saw you in the area last night. CDI Jones has some questions." Kato looked longingly at the glass of umeshu.

"Naruhodo." I said. Fukusawa just laughed.

"Officer Kato, keep an old lady company for a bit?" she said. Kato looked confused, then flustered. Fukusawa was hardly an old lady. She would get details out of Kato, he just didn't know it yet. Fukusawa knew everything that went on in our town.

"Great. While you keep my seat warm, I'll go talk with CDI Watanabe." I said. CDI Jones didn't like anyone calling him by his surname. Except me. I didn't know if that was a good thing or a bad thing. Probably both.

I got up and headed out of my office. The coffee shop was across the street from the koban. Few people came to this part of town anymore, not since the American Embassy closed up shop. The damage from the Drift and the 3rd Great Kanto Earthquake rendered many buildings in Tokyo unusable, including the American's Embassy. The coffee shop, however, was untouched and still made great bean juice.

THE ALIBI, THE RENTAL LAWYER, AND THE CONSEQUENCES

"CDI Watanabe, how can I help you today?" I asked as I sat down across from the detective in the coffee shop.

"Lejeune, glad you could make it. What did you do to my officer?" CDI Watanabe stared up at me over a steaming hot coffee.

"Nothing. My landlady is getting him drunk and pumping him for information." I said.

"Har-har. No, really, where's Kato?" The detective was also new to this koban. He didn't know that Fukusawa was likely doing exactly what I said she was doing.

"He's back at my office, probably making an illegal search for whatever evidence you asked him to plant." I said as I sat down. I waved to the camera and made the sign for green tea. Hopefully, my talent didn't break the closed circuit TV.

"Green tea? I thought a troubleshooter like you would go for solid, black coffee?" CDI Watanabe asked. He drank from his cup, slurping the hot bean juice.

"Not until nighttime. I only drink coffee at night." I said. Untrue, but what did the detective care?

"A man's dead. You do it, Lejeune?" The detective wasn't much for formality. Or tact.

"I don't kill people, CDI Watanabe. Kato said something about Toranomon Downs. Who died?" I asked.

"Local guy. We hear he owns one of those virtual experience places, a skinless brothel. You know anything about that?" The detective slurped more coffee and my green tea arrived with a waiter. I paid and took a long sip.

"Look, Lejeune. Zach. I know we got off on the wrong foot with that Rufus murder, but be straight with me, ok? I know you own Rufus' operation now and this guy was in the same business. I need to know you are clean." The CDI was throwing me a bone. Or a rope.

"Naruhodo." I said.

"Cut the crap. We found Iijima in a tank of mining slurry, half cooked and drown in the filth from excavating the old metro station. I don't have time for this and neither do you." CDI Watanabe must have been under pressure. No one gave away that much information unless they were stupid, drunk, or desperate. Of the two of us, I was only slightly inebriated.

"Naruhodo. I've never even heard of Iijima-san. Was he a local? And just so you know, I only just found out I owned Rufus' business this morning. How the hell did you know about it before me?" I emptied my green tea and gestured to the camera for more.

"What do you mean? They changed the signs on the place last week. 'The Zach Tragic Experience' went live four days ago. Of course you knew about that." The detective waved at the camera and yelled back to the kitchen, "More of this, please?"

Huh. Courtesy. Well, CDI 'Jones' Watanabe levels of courtesy. Interesting.

"Look, the government bengoshi just told me about it this morning. If anything, this is Saito-san's deal. He was my lawyer, he did the lien execution. He must have done the sign and the rest too." I said as I took my tea from the waiter.

"Excuse me." I looked up. It wasn't the waiter, it was the OL special from that morning. I looked down, it wasn't my tea. I handed the cup back to her.

"Sorry."

"It seems to me, you need a lawyer. And I just became available." OL special smiled and sipped at her cup.

"Look, lady, this is a private police conversation." CDI Watanabe was his normal, pleasant self.

"Konno-san, I thought you were with those other two government bengoshi?" I asked.

"My services were no longer required. I'm a rental." OL special said as she sipped.

Rental lawyers are the worst. Unable to hold down a regular position, usually due to being incompetent, rentals are the bane of the legal profession. Konno-san was young, dressed in the cheapest, first-job suit possible. She was rented and discarded by the up and coming razor-suit and the hereditary Savile Row spoiled brat. I was definitely in trouble.

"Sure, have a seat." I said, "CDI Watanabe, please meet my lawyer, Konno-san."

CDI Watanabe just shook his head. What did I have to lose? My talent didn't affect me, it only brought bad luck to those people and things around me. Maybe this was payback for CDI Watanabe beating the sense out of me when my previous lawyer set me up to take the fall for Rufus' murder? One could only hope.

"Konno-san, this is Chief Detective Inspector Watanabe Ichiro. Call him Jones unless you want a beating." I introduced my new rental lawyer to her opposition.

Konno put her teacup down and took a slim meishi case from her suit jacket's inner pocket. It was old and beautiful. The copper inside the case flashed red in the light as Konno opened the enameled lid. A crane and a dragon if I was wasn't mistaken. Interesting and definitely not something a typical rental lawyer could afford.

The meishi was presented by Konno with grace. CDI Watanabe snapped it from her hands in the rudest way possible. It was a step up for the detective.

"Charmed, I'm sure. Call me CDI Jones. Never call me Watanabe. No one does." CDI Watanabe said as he examined the card. I could swear his eyes got softer as he rubbed the paper between his thumb and forefinger. Very interesting.

"My client does." Konno said as she took a seat from the next table and sat facing us both.

"What? Oh. Zach has permission. You don't." he said, "Now, to business. Were you in Toranomon Downs last night, Mr. Lejeune?"

I paused and looked at my new rental OL special. She made a slow blink, which I interpreted as permission to speak. I may not like lawyers, but I know how they work.

"Yes. I was with a client. We were at nomikai to celebrate the conclusion of our work." I said.

"And this client, what was his name?" CDI Watanabe asked.

"Matsumoto. Matsumoto Reiko is her name." I answered.

"What's she do? Work in your new skinless? Or are you branching out into the illegal kind of work?" The detective was relentless and about as subtle as a double-barreled shotgun.

"You don't have to answer that question, Mr. Lejeune." My OL special said. She was right, never answer a leading question. Maybe she was not a cheap rental after all.

"Matsumoto-san is in the fruit import business. She is worth more than you, me, and my esteemed counsel put together. No offense." I said to Konno-san.

"None taken." Konno said without missing a beat.

"What did you do for Matsumoto, the fruit girl?" CDI Watanabe asked.

"Matsumoto-san is the Chief Technical Officer for Yokoso Fruits. She has a new automated import line. It vacuums up the fruit and packages it. Clockwork. No micros. Matsumoto-san wanted to know if it had any faults or failure modes. I found them, and she fixed them. Equitable arrangement for everyone." I said, dropping the right names to impress CDI Watanabe and my new lawyer.

"Yokoso Fruits. Matsumoto the horologist? You worked for her and you expect me to believe she took you to a dive like Toranomon Downs? Why not the Kin Gai? Why not Fujiisan, for crying out loud?" CDI Watanabe's voice cracked. Matsumoto Reiko was a common enough name. Matsumoto the horologist was the one and only person of her kind. An authentic genius of clockwork mechanisms. Everyone knew her name and her reputation. That reputation was not made on Toranomon Downs.

"I don't care what you believe, Ichiro. I was at a drinking party. I don't kill people." I said.

"How did you get home?" CDI Watanabe was not happy, but at least he wasn't trying to give me a couple lumps to go with my hangover.

I glanced at Konno. She gave me the slow blink.

"I walked to my office. Around 2 or 3 in the morning." I said.

"Walked by the excavation site?" Watanabe asked.

"I think so. I was drunk. That's what happens at a nomikai." I said.

"Right past the slurry tanks?" The detective said.

"I dunno. Nomikai. In the dark. What's a slurry tank?" The detective annoyed me, so I played dumb.

"It's where they dump the hot waste from the drill heads excavating the old metro station. Water, stone, dirt. All of it boiling hot from the friction of the excavation and drilling. That's why Iijima was cooked. Until I get a better alibi from you or someone confesses, stay in town, Zach." Watanabe finished his coffee, stood, and walked out.

"I think that went well. I'll send my invoice, Lejeune-sama. See you in the morning? Ready to discuss your case?" Konno stood. Her OL special seemed to fit a little better.

"My office. Don't come earlier than 10 in the morning." I said, "And thanks. I appreciate your effort."

"Don't say that until you see the bill, Lejeune-sama." The OL special smiled.

THE EMPLOYEES, THE LANDLADY,
AND THE WAGER

I slept at my office again. That was a mistake.

The loud voices and banging at my door woke me from a sound sleep. I couldn't really make out what they were saying, but I could tell it was nothing good. I knew I needed to just keep quiet until they left. I don't get a lot of disgruntled clients, but when I do, they are usually extremely disgruntled.

My business is very specialized. My clients want to improve their business, make sure they are risking as little as possible. My job is to discover the risks. My talent makes this a unique proposition. I am a sink for bad luck, a corollary to Murphy's Law. Murphy's Law states that anything that can go wrong, will go wrong. The corollary is 'usually when Zach Lejeune is around.' My nickname reflects that truth. Zach Tragic. Bad things happen when I'm around. Nothing that wouldn't happen anyway, I just tip the scales of chance towards that bad thing happening right then and there.

Sometimes, a client takes that bad thing, that tragic occurrence, personally. It isn't me; it isn't my fault, but they don't see it that way. I have a reinforced door in a solid concrete building for those times when a client takes it personally.

Unfortunately, my door is not immune to my talent. The lock, specifically, was not immune to breaking at the worst time. The door burst open, and although it didn't hit me when the striker for the lock snapped and flew across the room, it scared the crap out of me. I didn't have enough time to think about it because of the half-dozen rough-looking men and women that flooded my office, grabbed me, and slammed me up against the wall.

"Hajimemashita?" I said, trying to defuse the situation. I had no idea who these people were.

One of the tougher-looking women responded with a baseball bat to my stomach. Not unreasonable, I guess.

"Shut up, Tragic, you murdering bastard." she said. Why did everyone think I was a murderer? I hardly ever kill anything larger than a bottle of umeshu. Occasionally some sake. Never shochu, that stuff rips me up.

I tried to follow the yelling and accusations. I couldn't.

"He was a good boss, what did he ever do to you?" Someone yelled.

"You bastard, I only had a week left on my contract." A man in the back shouted, spitting as he yelled.

"Iijima-san was like a father. A crazy, perverted father, but that was better than my real one." A woman in the middle shouted while crying crocodile tears. Iijima-san. Why was that name familiar? Oh, yeah. The dead man in the slurry. Just my luck.

"Naruhodo." I said between blows from the woman with the bat. She was not trying to kill me, but it still hurt like hell. My ears rang, and the ringing got louder. I could tell it was really bad when the half-dozen morons beating the crap out of me heard the ringing in my ears as well.

"Next one who hits my tenant gets dead, fast." I heard Fukusawa shout over the ear piercing tone cutting through the air. I could see her in the doorway over the head of the tough woman with the bat. Fukusawa's arm was slit open down its length and a strange green glow came from inside the prosthetic.

Huh. Maybe the rumors about her were right? Who knows?

"Fukusawa the knife?" One moron said. They knew the rumors.

"Yeah, that's me and if you know that, you know not to mess with my people." Fukusawa stepped into the room and raised her artificial arm towards the crowd. They ran. Fast. My office emptied until it was just me, Fukusawa the knife and the baseball bat woman.

Baseball bat woman looked like she would try to take Fukusawa. I leaned on the wall to keep standing. My ribs hurt.

"Terrible idea, girlfriend." Fukusawa said. The baseball bat hit the floor, and the woman ran out past my landlady.

"Thanks." I said when I could get enough breath and energy to speak.

"You're paying for the door." Fukusawa said as her arm sealed back up. It looked like a normal artificial arm again, no weird glow, no ringing sound.

"Naruhodo." I said.

"Why is Iijima Kyosuke's staff trying to kill you, Zach?" Fukusawa helped me into my office chair. She ignored the thin pad I had been sleeping on before the attack.

"You know them? I have no idea who they are or why

they want to kill me. Iijima, you say? The police said he was dead. Who is he?" I said, trying to get my thoughts together.

"He runs a sketchy skinless like your friend Rufus did. Dead, you say? I hadn't heard that." Fukusawa said as she looked at my ribs under my shirt. She pushed gently, and it hurt. Something was definitely not right.

"Feels like something is cracked." My landlady said.

"You can tell that?" I asked.

"No. I just want you to go to the doctor, even though I know you won't." She was right.

"What was that sound? It was like a ringing or a tone?" I winced as Fukusawa prodded me.

"Oh, that? Emergency siren in my arm. I have it for when the next quake comes. I won't get trapped under the building." she said.

"Didn't sound like a siren." I replied.

"Yeah, if I don't give it enough power, it just sort of whines and whimpers. Kinda like you, Zach-chan." Fukusawa was enjoying my pain. I smiled.

"You forgot to charge the arm, again?" I asked.

"Not this time, but that is how I found out it could annoy people enough to make them behave. It's better than thumping morons." Fukusawa smiled.

"Thanks. I think I need to get down to Toranomon. I'll go see a doctor after I see what Rufus got me into from beyond the grave."

"So dramatic, Zach-chan." Fukusawa teased me, "You should take a precaution or two."

Fukusawa was right, and I knew it. I opened a drawer and took out an extreme *precaution*. I placed the *precaution* in the pocket of my vest and asked my landlady to help me put in on over my ribs. It hurt.

After she left, I got myself together and headed down

the street. Toranomon Downs was a quick walk away. The area had been a business and government section of Tokyo before the 3rd Great Kanto Earthquake. The buildings were not the largest skyscrapers or the most modern architectures, but the thirty or so blocks that made up Toranomon were wealthy and well-developed. The collapse of the metro under Toranomon ended all that. The giant, gaping subsidence that opened up swallowed entire buildings, including the jewel of the town, Toranomon Heights. The largest building there was damaged beyond repair, and the rest of the neighborhood was not far behind.

I headed toward Toranomon 41. They named building addresses in Forgotten Tokyo in the order of construction. Toranomon 1 would be the first building built in the town. Rufus' skinless brothel was in Toranomon 41, one of the last buildings completed before the Drift and the Earthquake. We talk about the two disasters about as if they were interchangeable, but they weren't. The Drift was first, and it rendered modern technology unreliable and advanced tech became worthless overnight. That was the beginning of the Forgetting. Seven years later, the 3rd Great Kanto Earthquake hit and Tokyo became Forgotten Tokyo to the rest of the world. We weren't important anymore without the internet, telecommunications, and the tech that had made Tokyo the heart of the world in the 21st Century.

Rufus' business, The Blind Kiwi, was in one of the last buildings that had the modern infrastructure needed to support a virtual experience. Even though most electronics and microprocessor based technology was unreliable with the new, shifting electromagnetic fields caused by the Drift, heavily shielded tech was fairly resilient. Toranomon 41 was a very well built, shielded building.

Until the fire, that is. Rufus had taxed the electrical

supply and wiring in Toranomon 41 to the limit, and the place had burned. The bones of the building were still good, but Rufus had been deep in debt and repairs cost money. Then my lawyer poisoned him with a fugu liver laced onigiri. I wasn't sure what I would find when I got to the dive.

I stopped outside The Blind Kiwi and just stared. I had brought the baseball bat with me as a second precaution. The morons had been from one of Rufus' competitors and I didn't really need another beating. I almost dropped the bat as I looked up at the garish neon sign on the still charred facade of Toranomon 41. It read *The Zach Tragic Experience.* Simply lovely.

"Naruhodo." I said.

"Like your new place, Mr. Lejeune?" A familiar voice said from just behind me.

"Oh, I don't know. Could use a bit of paint. Maybe something in British Racing Green?" I said and turned to face Savile Row and placed my left hand into my vest pocket while I held the bat with my right.

"Well said. British sensibilities are important." Savile Row said, caressing the fine cloth of his suit. No doubt he caught my meaning.

"What are you doing here, bengoshi?" I asked.

"Lawyer? Bengoshi, is it? I know that rental gave you my card. You should know my name." Savile Row said, working at loosening his French cuffs. His wrists were red, and he seemed uncomfortable. Maybe the burn was starting to peel?

"Yeah, I couldn't care less what your name is." I said honestly.

"Well, my friend here would like to have a word with

you. And I have a proposition. A wager, if you like." Savile Row was annoying. He must have planned it.

"Is that so? What did you have in mind?" I clicked the button on my precaution and hefted the bat, my second precaution.

Savile Row stepped aside and the tough woman from my office stepped out of the doorway across the street from Toranomon 41. I let my grip go loose on her bat. She held a sledgehammer with a long haft. I guess she traded up.

"I represent Iijima-san's employees. They would like to punish you for killing their boss." Savile Row spoke while tough woman twisted her hands as she gripped the sledge-hammer. Lovely.

"I didn't kill Iijima. I didn't even know him." I said.

"They feel differently. You are the competition, with Iijima gone, they are out of business and you are in. Your lawyer, Saito-sama, made sure Iijima knew you were the new boss. Seems convenient Iijima got offed in the slurry tank." Savile Row was smiling. Definitely a set up.

"You dumped the boss in the slurry tanks?" Tough woman said, "Cops didn't tell me that. I don't care about the brothel, I want your head." she said, pointing her hammer at my head for emphasis. She used only one hand to lift the tool. Her strength was obvious.

"So what is this wager?" I asked, wanting this to be over.

"Iijima's kohai her wants your head. I want the busi-ness. If she beats you, I take *The Zach Tragic Experience* and you get to live." It was clear now what this was all about. I tossed the bat to the ground.

"Fine."

THE FIGHT, THE RECORDER, AND
THE LAWYER

"HOLD STILL YOU SON-OF-A-BITCH." THE TOUGH woman yelled as I sidestepped another swing from her sledgehammer.

"I would rather you didn't hit me with that hammer. It seems a bit much." I said. She circled me as we stood in the middle of the road.

"Shut up and let me hit you." She said. Sweat was covering her face and getting in her eyes. I kicked the baseball bat away from me. Best not to let her think I was trying to trip her up. My talent would take care of that, eventually.

The woman changed her grip on the haft of the sledgehammer. She spread her hands apart, giving her less power but more control over the tool. I guess she was more than just a thug. She knew how to use the hammer, but did she know how to use it as a weapon?

"Why don't we go play pachinko for the wager instead? Doesn't that sound nice?" I suggested.

"I don't get to break your face playing pachinko." The woman said.

"And I don't get to watch her break your face, Mr. Lejeune." Savile Row added.

"What do you care, bengoshi? I only met you yesterday. What do you have against me?" I asked, genuinely curious why Savile Row would even care.

"Well, you did business with my cousin. It didn't turn out well for him." Savile Row said.

"Naruhodo." I said, dodging a thrust from the tough woman's hammer. The extra control her grip gave her was making the fight harder. She was getting closer, and it was only a matter or time before she landed a blow.

"Hold still, scarecrow. I need to make you pay." she said.

"You're a family lawyer, right? A legacy?" I needed to draw this out. I suspected this was all a frame. I needed to prove it.

"How could you tell? Three generations in the public service." Savile Row said, fluffing his suit jacket in pride. I could see the fabric was getting thin. Wealthy enough for an English style suit from actual England. Not wealthy enough to replace it from when grandfather wore it.

"Is that Tsugaru-ben? You from up north?" I said, making a wild guess.

"Hardly. It's Akita-ben. Still up north, but not one of those country folk up in Aomori." Gotchya, Savile Row.

"Stop talking and die, already." Tough woman yelled after a spectacular miss that kicked up sparks off the road where the sledgehammer head hit.

"Must be nice this time of year. Cool, pleasant. Not like the sweltering summers here in Tokyo." I said.

"Who can afford to go back to the country? I know I look like money, but I prefer to keep it, not spend it." Savile Row said, offended.

"Hey, I'm broke half the time too. I bet this lovely lady

trying to kill me is, too. Are you broke today?" I asked, touching the hammer head and giving it a little push as she swung it past my head. Tough woman stumbled with the extra momentum I had given her. She slipped on the base-ball bat and went down in a heap. My talent was very useful in a fight.

"Yeah. I'm broke, but not as broke as you will be when I get my hands on you." she said from the ground.

"Miki, can you wrap this up?" Savile Row said to the tough woman.

"He's slippery and hard to hit. So thin, he has to be bouncing on the wind. I can't get a hit in." Miki said.

"You want a fighting chance, Miki?" I said, "Leave the hammer, just come at me."

"Don't say my name. Iijima-sempai was worth ten of you. He trained me and that training will take you down." Miki said as she stood and squared off with me. She left the hammer on the ground. Interesting.

"Fine. Iijima-san trained you?" I said as Miki swung a competent jab at my face. Boxing. Great.

"What of it? He liked to fight. I like to fight." Miki swung a left, testing my movements. I weaved and stepped back.

"Coward." she said.

"Iijima-san. Was he a big man?" I asked.

"Big enough. Short and thick. He could squish you like a bug." Miki said as she closed and threw a serious left and followed with her right coming in low for my face.

I stepped into her and the left went past me while her right got caught up in my vest. I was too close for her to connect with power. I whispered to Miki something only she could hear.

"Come on. He's a punk. Finish this Miki." Savile Row was impatient.

We broke. Miki pushed me away with force. Disgust twisted her face. I had gotten to her. Good.

"Bengoshi. Your cousin was my lawyer, Saito-san. Wasn't he?" I said.

"So what if he was?" Savile Row shouted back. Miki paced, sizing me up.

"Saito-san put the lien on Rufus' place. He arranged for the neon sign, *The Zach Tragic Experience*, right?" I spoke loud, slightly out of breath.

"So what?"

"So you represented Iijima-san, and now you represent his employees?" I asked.

"I did, and I do." Savile Row confirmed.

"And now Saito-san is in jail after trying to murder me. He tried to get Rufus' business on a lien I had no idea existed. But you did. You and your cousin."

"That doesn't mean a thing, Mr. Lejeune. Try harder." The strain was in his voice.

"Doesn't it? Iijima was a boxer if I read Miki's moves right. A good one if he trained her." I said.

"He was. A champion, once." Miki said.

"He would have eaten me alive the other night. I was stumbling blind drunk after a nomikai." I said.

"You must have gotten a lucky shot. They don't call you Zach Tragic for nothing. People end up dead around you. Things go bad." Savile Row said.

"No. It doesn't work like that. Things go bad, but they don't drown men in slurry. Hot, scalding slurry." I said.

"You got lucky, then." He said.

"How are those burns on your arms, bengoshi?" I spat the words out fast. He took the bait. Said nothing. He knew

I had seen them under the French cuffs. A full Savile Row suit in the Tokyo summer? It wasn't vanity, Savile Row was covering up the evidence.

"That so, Mr. Ito?" Miki asked in a loud voice.

"He's a liar." Savile Row protested.

"Show me your arms, Mr. Ito?" Miki asked.

"I don't have to show you anything, net-scum." Mistake number one.

"Show me your arms, Mr. Ito." Miki insisted.

"I don't answer to you, woman. Iijima didn't play ball after Saito got nicked. You play ball now, or I'll have your head." Mistake number two.

I stepped on the end of the baseball bat and tipped the end up. I flicked my other toe under it and kicked it up, catching it in the air.

"Miki-sama, I think this is yours?" I said, offering the bat to my former opponent.

"I can take it from here, Mr. Lejeune. Thanks." Miki said as she walked towards Savile Row. His face showed he realized his mistakes. Not all lawyers are clever or quick. Savile Row was a little clever, but not at all quick.

I reached into my vest pocket and clicked off the digital recorder. I had enough to clear my name. Fifteen minutes later, Miki returned with a broken baseball bat.

"What now?" I asked.

"I don't know, but you were right. You couldn't have killed Iijima-san. You're good, but he was better." Miki said.

"And I was dead drunk."

"How did you know Mr. Ito was behind it? The murder and everything?" Miki asked.

"Too many coincidences. Things never line up like that unless something's wrong. Framing me for Iijima-san's death? Suddenly gaining Rufus' business on a lien I never filed? From my lawyer from Akita. And this lawyer, with burns on his arms? Who was from Akita? A family legacy and my lawyer's cousin. Everyone is the right place at the right time. Nothing is ever that convenient when I'm involved. I have a talent for things going wrong." I mused.

"Well, I am out of a job now. Iijima's place was in debt to that creep lawyer." Miki said.

"He called you net-scum. You a sysadmin?" I asked.

"Yeah. I got a brain *and* muscles." Miki replied.

"I know a guy who has a virtual experience business and doesn't know what to do about it. You have any experience in that field?" I asked, knowing the answer.

"I might. Want to introduce me to your guy?" Miki replied, smiling.

"Let's grab a beer. We can talk while we drink."

I GOT BACK to my office around noon. Konno-san was waiting for me in my office chair. She didn't look furious, but looks are deceiving. I sat in the chair for clients.

"Nice of you to keep our 10 o'clock, Mr. Lejeune." Konno-san said. A lawyer with sarcasm in her arsenal. Just what I needed after a three beer lunch.

"Sorry. Some folks tried to kill me. It didn't take." I said as I tossed my digital recorder on the desk.

"What's this?" Konno asked, arching her eyebrow up.

"Confession. Savile Row set me up for Iijima's murder." I said.

"Naruhodo." Konno said.

"That's my line. I'll send you an invoice for doing your job." I smiled.

"Naruhodo." Konno smiled back.

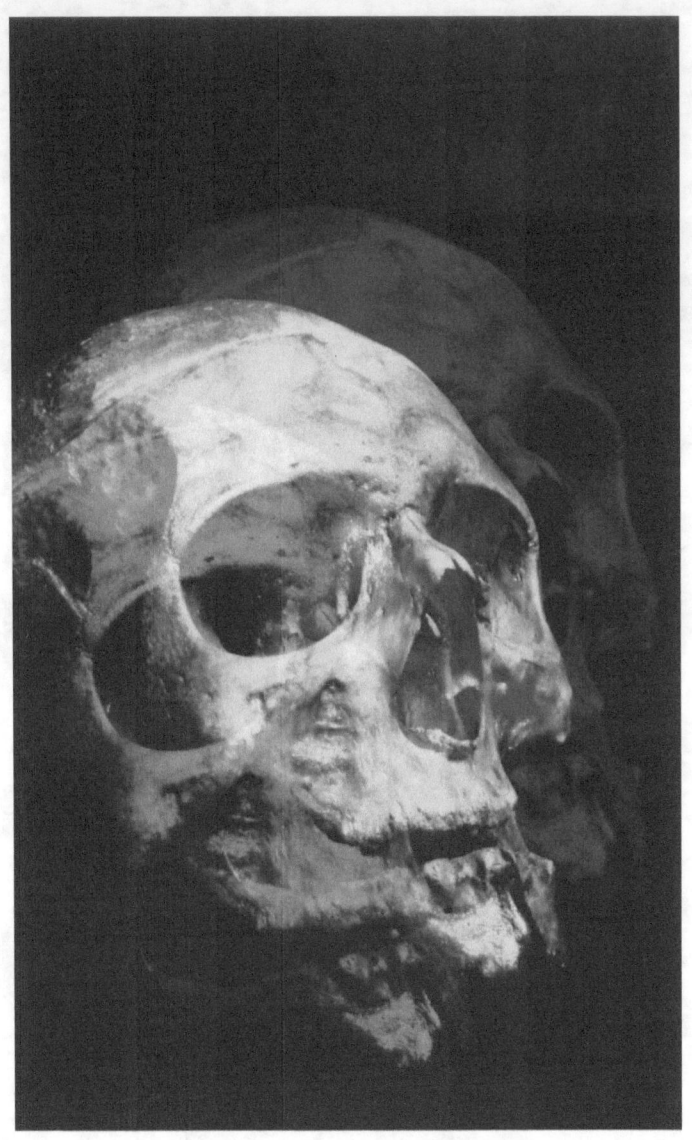

3

TRAGIC AND THE BODY

THE BUSINESS, THE FIRE, AND
THE BODY

"Miki-san, why am I here?" I asked the stout boxer who was also my new business manager. Miki looked directly at me and repeatedly clenched and unclenched her jaw.

"Because, Mr. Tragic, we are having a work impasse at your business and I need you to step in and resolve it for me." Miki said, grabbing my arm and dragging me into the still scorched Toranomon 41 building.

Miki was shorter than me but built tough in all the places I was lank and spindly. We made an unlikely couple and an even more unlikely set of business partners. There was no romantic relationship, but even our friendship seemed odd to the people working at 'The Zach Tragic Experience.'

"Miki, please call me Zach, or Mr. Lejeune. I disdain 'Zach Tragic.'" I said as Miki pulled me behind her into the first floor office. The fire at Toranomon 41 had left the main office untouched. I could not say the same for the upper and lower floors where the fire had started, grew, and then spread through the building using the elevator shaft and improvised electrical cabling as a pathway. I had only just gotten the last of the workers out of the blaze before it engulfed the entire second floor in flames.

"As long as your name is on the building, you're Zach Tragic to me, Mr. Lejeune." Miki smiled and forced me down to sit on a waiting office chair.

"Wakabayashi-san, I need you now." Miki called as she sat behind the manager's desk.

A meek little man entered the office. Wakabayashi Satoshi had been the lead technician for the Blind Kiwi, the virtual experience business that I had inherited from my deceased client, Nakajima 'Rufus' Amaro. Rufus had been done in by my former lawyer, one Mr. Saito. Shortly afterwards, a competitor of Rufus' turned up dead. They found Iijima Kyosuke half-cooked and entirely drown in a slurry tank near the excavation site of the old Toranomon Metro station.

Another bengoshi, Saito's cousin, had tried to frame me for Iijima's murder. Miki, who had been an employee and the kohai of Iijima, attempted to beat me to a bloody pulp in revenge. Instead of dying reasonably, I uncovered the actual killer. Mr. Ito, a legacy lawyer in fancy clothes, had conspired with his cousin, Mr. Saito, to corner the virtual experience business in Toranomon Downs. Instead of making a wagon-load of money and sending me to jail, Mr. Ito ended up having a violent disagreement with a baseball bat and a sufficiently motivated Miki. Afterwards, I made Miki a job offer to help me run the Blind Kiwi, now named 'The Zach Tragic Experience.'

I have issues working with technology. Things tend to break in my presence.

"Miki." Wakabayashi-san said. His voice was much deeper than his small body seemed to allow for.

"Wakabayashi." Miki replied.

"Naruhodo." I could tell this would be a tedious conversation.

"Please tell Mr. Tragic why you can't operate the systems?" Miki stared at Wakabayashi.

"Mr. Tragic, please ignore this person. She doesn't understand our business and how we are successful." Wakabayashi ignored Miki and looked at the floor under my chair. Introvert. Extreme introvert.

"On the contrary, I have worked sysadmin in a skinless brothel for seven years. I understand quite well how the business works." Miki stared at Wakabayashi, flexing her jaw.

"There is that word again. We are an experience business, not what you called us." Wakabayashi shifted his gaze to the space under Miki's desk.

"Look, just because you are a sexless 'NEET' doesn't mean the rest of us are as prudish as you. Call it whatever you want, a skinless brothel is still a brothel even if it is all in the bits." Miki's voice rose. I squirmed uncomfortably in my seat. I knew this argument had happened before. Probably daily since Miki arrived at Toranomon 41.

"We do not have sex related content. I keep telling you this, Miki-sama. We provide a different cut of experience than your Iijima-san did over at his place." I noticed Wakabayashi looked up as far as Miki's forearms. Perhaps not a fully introverted NEET.

"I don't get it. Sex, no sex. Who cares? Why does that mean we can't operate the systems?" I asked as Miki threw eye daggers at Wakabayashi.

"We need cleaning supplies and water." Miki said.

"We need nothing of the sort, we need flowers." Wakabayashi countered.

"I do not understand." I said.

"People are filthy." Miki said.

"We don't have that content." Wakabayashi yelled.

"Flowers?" Zach asked.

"For the obasans." Wakabayashi said as if it was obvious.

"Excuse me?" said a woman from the office entrance.

"Not now!" Miki and Wakabayashi said in unison.

"The door. I opened it." The woman said.

"What?" Wakabayashi was shocked. I had no idea why or what door was being talked about.

"I think you should come and see."

"Anything is better than this argument. I'm going to go see what is behind door number one." I said, getting up out of my chair and walking out of the office.

"Mr. Lejeune, I remember you. You were here when the fire broke out." The woman said.

"I was. Up on the second floor, where it started. Where were you?" I replied.

"I was in the VR closet, you pulled me out before the flames got too high." I looked at the woman closer. She was wearing clothes for cleaning, but if she was the person I remembered, she had been dressed in a full kimono when I found her in the VR closet.

"Are you the new VR operator? The one in the kimono? Tanaka, wasn't it? Tanaka Ai?" I asked, digging into my memory.

"Yes, that's me. The VR sysop," Tanaka-san said as she led me down into the basement, "Here we are."

A darkened, charred metal door was open. The lock was cut out of the door, and a plasma torch was sitting nearby. I walked around the door and looked into the room beyond. A body was leaning against the back wall, a thoroughly burned and quite deceased corpse. The light from the basement was just enough to show the body but not enough to show everything. I gestured to Tanaka-san for the flashlight in her hand.

I shined the light on the corpse. Metal glittered under the blackened skin of the body's head. The site was horrific.

"Better call CDI Jones." I said, "but call Konno Asuka right after that. I think we need my new lawyer."

"What is it?" Miki said as she and Wakabayashi came down the steps and rounded the door to stand next to me.

"A problem."

"Understatement, Mr. Lejeune." Wakabayashi said.

"Wait until the police see this." Miki added.

"WHY DO I only ever get to talk to you over a body, Lejeune?" Chief Detective Inspector Watanabe 'Jones' Ichiro said to me as he looked over the burned corpse in the basement of 'The Zach Tragic Experience.'

"Don't answer that, Mr. Lejeune." Konno, Asuka said.

"Wasn't planning on it." I replied.

"Well, we need the doctors and the lab techs. The portable forensic unit can't handle this. Officer Kato, get this taken care of, all right?" CDI Jones said to his subordinate.

"Koban?" I asked.

"Koban," CDI Jones confirmed, "All of you."

We walked up the stairs and out of the basement. The Akasaka koban was only a few minutes away from Toranomon 41. We passed a woman my age or so coming in as we left.

"Hello, Wakabayashi-san," she said.

"Oh, hello, Matsumoto-sama," Wakabayashi said to the woman as he passed her in the entrance. Her arms were full of three massive bouquets of wild flowers, "Just leave the flowers in the office, if you would?"

"Of course. Did something happen? Why are there so many police here today?" Matsumoto-sama asked.

"Obasan, not now." CDI Jones was unduly rude. Although Matsumoto-sama was somewhere in her forties like me, I considered rude to address her as 'obasan.'

Matsumoto ignored the detective. Wakabayashi stopped and placed a hand on Matsumoto-sama's shoulder.

"Please, don't worry. They found something in that old locked room in the basement. Behind the metal door." Wakabayashi said.

"Enough. Let's go, tech-boy." CDI Jones had a special way with rudeness.

"Oh." Matsumoto-sama said, looking especially grim as she walked into Toranomon 41 with her armfuls of fresh flowers.

"What does a skinless need with flowers?" CDI Jones muttered as they walked towards Akasaka.

"Another one of you? We are not one of those places. I'll have you know that our ikebana experience is almost as popular as our gardening set course of virtual experiences. We are not a filthy trade." Wakabayashi said.

"He's not wrong, you know. Rufus had a soft spot for ikebana. The VR unit was for tea ceremony." I said.

"Wait, you mean the pencil-neck was serious? You knew about this, Tragic?" Miki asked. Judging from her expression, she thought Wakabayashi had been lying.

"Of course. Rufus' customers were usually in their sixth or seventh decade. Lots of money to relive the good old days. That's how he could afford me to troubleshoot the

Blind Kiwi when he bought that VR set-up. Why do you ask?" I played dumb.

"Well, I'll be damned. I guess I'm glad I never patronized his place before it burned. That would have been a tremendous disappointment, if you get my meaning." CDI Jones said.

"No one wants to get your meaning, Jones. No one." Konno said.

THE LAWYER, THE DRIFT, AND THE RUMOR

"I think we are getting ahead of ourselves, don't you, CDI Jones?" My lawyer was talking. I just listened. Most lawyers in Forgotten Tokyo are useless. The rental lawyers are even worse. Konno Asuka was a rental lawyer when I met her, but she was different. There are a few great, independent bengoshi, and Konno was one of them.

"I don't care, lady," CDI Jones wasn't shouting yet.

"Konno-sama, if you please."

"Konno-san. Look, every time I deal with your client it is because there is a dead body. Why is that?" CDI Jones said, leaning in to get right under my lawyer's face. Konno didn't seem to either notice nor care.

"Maybe if you did your job better, my client wouldn't have to clean up your mess." I really liked my lawyer.

"Now you listen here, Konno-san, I will not take that disrespect in my koban." Jones yelled. I watched the exchange from a folding chair outside the koban. Jones had banned me from the inside of the building. My former lawyer, a Mr. Saito, had tried to frame me, poison the cops, and then kill me with CDI Jones' own revolver. The detective didn't let me enter the koban after that. Bad luck, he said. I didn't mind.

"And I, my good detective, will not tolerate your baseless accusations against my client." Konno said as she stood and turned on her heel.

"Where are you going?" Jones asked.

"Until you have the results of the forensic scans and autopsy, my client and I are going back to his office. You can find us there when you need to apologize in person." Konno said as she walked away from the detective. Looking at her in her Office Lady special suit, you could be forgiven for thinking she was just a beginning bengoshi. Jones knew better. There were bruises.

"Fine. I still have to talk with your employees. They better vouch for you, Tragic." Jones yelled at me.

"Come on, Mr. Lejeune. We are leaving." she said as she walked past me. I got up and folded the chair, placing it just inside the koban.

"Counselor, you are amazing." I said as I walked just behind my lawyer.

"I know. Tell me more and see if it reduces your invoice."

"I know better than that, counselor." I said as we walked the rest of the way in silence. My office was less than five minutes from the Akasaka koban by foot.

Officer Kato ran past us as we crossed the street in front of the old newspaper building. Konno stopped him with a look and her hand barely brushed his chest as she raised it with her fingers spread wide. Kato broke his run to avoid touching Konno-sama. She had that effect on him. Love or fear. Probably both.

"Officer Kato, how *are* you today?" Konno started wrapping the young officer around her finger.

"Aye-aye, ma'am. I am well, and how are you, Ms. Konno-sama?" Kato was like a small puppy, layering both the English and the Japanese honorifics on his greeting.

"I am healthy and happy. Where are you heading with such haste?" Ouch. Fancy words from a bengoshi are a bad sign when those words are directed at you. I felt for Kato.

"Results are in from the autopsy. It's incredible. The body is male. From before the 3rd Great Kanto Earthquake. Maybe even from the Drift." Kato was breathless, yet spewed out a mass of words to Konno-sama.

"Oh, really? What do you mean, Officer Kato?" My lawyer continued, "The body is from the time of the Drift?"

"Oh, yes. Maybe even deceased during the Drift itself. Can you imagine that? The biggest magnetic aberration in the planet's history, and your man died during it! I read about the fatalities in school, people with intense electronic implants, smart pacemakers, in-head keitai. But I have never seen one outside of a book." Kato was exuberant. I envied him that kind of childish indulgence.

"Oh, really?" My counselor said.

"Naruhodo." I muttered.

"Shh, the adults are talking, Mr. Lejeune. Go on, Officer Kato?" I shut up.

"The body, the young man, really, because he was young. In his twenties, perhaps?" Officer Kato was rambling from excitement.

"Yes, what about the body, please tell me more?" I listened to Konno-san wrap Kato tighter around her fingers.

"The body? Right, he was burned to death by his own electronics. There was almost a half a kilogram of slagged electronic implants in his head. Almost like a fully cyber-netic science fiction robot." Kato said. Implants and subcu-taneous electronics ceased being viable after the Drift. The body was unlikely to date from much after that singular event. The risk for anyone was too great. No one wanted to be fried by their built-in telephone or office email implant. Not that email was a thing anymore than telecommunications networks. After the Drift, almost everything reverted to simple, non-integrated circuit systems.

"So interesting, Officer Kato. You should run and tell CDI Jones everything. He will be so delighted to know that my client had no involvement with this person's death." I love my lawyer in a platonic and professional way. I have seen her invoices.

"Aye-aye! Right away, ma'am." Officer Kato ran off to the koban.

"Now, let's get you out of here before your detective friend comes to beat you up for letting me compromise his Officer and his investigation." Konno didn't wait for me to reply before walking off.

"You weren't responsible for that man's death, were you, Mr. Lejeune?" Konno asked as I followed her.

"Of course not. I was in Sumida. At Skytree." I said.

"That is an air-tight alibi. Not even CDI Jones will try to mess with that, would he?" Konno knew the answer. Anyone alive and when the Drift hit Tokyo knew about Skytree. A few knew I was there. Most people think everyone died. We weren't that lucky.

My landlady, Fukusawa, was waiting for us when we topped the steps to the second floor of her building. It was my office, but Fukusawa owned the entire structure outright.

"What's this I hear about you burning bodies, Zach-chan?" she said as my lawyer and I stopped to chat. Fukusawa knows all the good rumors in town. It's not why they call her Fukusawa the Knife, but that hardly matters.

"One employee at Rufus' place found a body behind that old locked door in the basement." I said.

"I heard you desecrated a grave and set the body on fire. And the building. But since I know Rufus' place burned months ago, I knew something was wrong. I figured something must be up." Fukusawa casually inserted a socket wrench into her right arm. It was a prosthetic arm and state-of-the-art a decade back.

"I could believe that, from the Nogitsune of Sumida." Konno-sama said. Sometimes, I hate my lawyer and I shot her a look to let her know I wasn't pleased. Konno Asuka smiled.

"Counselor. Thank you for that colorful reminder of my alibi." I said, "Please remember to deduct it from your charges."

"Trouble in paradise, lovers?" Fukusawa chided.

"Ha! Now that is funny." Konno said.

"You know me better than that, Fukusawa-san." I wasn't thrilled to get the verbal jabs from both sides at once.

"Then why bring up Sumida? Unless you want Zach here to fire you and your considerable services?" Fukusawa ignored me and talked to my lawyer.

"It's his alibi. The body was burned up during the Drift, or damn close to it." she said.

"Now isn't that interesting. I hadn't heard that." My landlady said, turning the wrench in her arm.

"Yeah, I was busy with trying to stay alive and not letting anyone else die." I walked to my office door and unlocked it. The shiny, new bolt on the opposite side clicked open. Miki and a mob of former employees of Iijima had busted my door down and tried to kill me. The new bolt was compliments of Fukusawa.

"I think I will have a talk with some of the old ladies

around here. Sato-san, Oota-san, and Matsumoto-san all lived around this area back then. Maybe they know something? Although I think one or another of them might be the source of the rumors." Fukusawa smiled at me as I walked into my office, leaving her and my lawyer behind.

"You do that. I will see if I have any work. I need to do something unrelated to dead things." I said as the door closed behind me.

Nogitsune of Sumida. The wild fox of Sumida. It was a nickname I wasn't proud of and never wanted to hear again. How the hell Konno Asuka knew it and knew it applied to me was a mystery. I guess that is how I knew she was an excellent lawyer. Sometimes I don't know if I hate or love my lawyer. Probably both.

THE OPINION, THE RUMORS, AND
THE BROTHER

"WHAT DO YOU MEAN, I CAN'T HAVE THE REPORT?" I asked my lawyer. Konno Asuka had stopped by my office first thing in the morning with the unwelcome news.

"The police will not release the report. In case of legal action." she said.

"Really? Who am I going to sue? The corpse? Thank you for dying 17 years ago in my building. Please pay me damages for your untimely demise?" I was not happy, and I chose my words accordingly.

"I would not advise that course of action, Mr. Lejeune." she said.

"I can't tell if you are being sarcastic or serious, counselor." I replied.

"You'll know when you get my invoice." she said.

"All right. This is getting us nowhere. The entire conversation is monotonous. Do you have anything useful to tell me, or was this visit just to pad the bill?" I asked, letting my exasperation show.

"I wanted you to know, I could not find any information on the deceased. The records from before the earthquake are hit or miss. I will keep trying, but you should know that I am not likely to turn up anything we don't already know." Konno said. I wasn't terribly surprised. The Great Kanto Earthquake in 1923 had destroyed much of Tokyo and burned Sumida and Yokohama to the ground. The 3rd Great Kanto Earthquake was not as destructive, but the human toll was much greater. Over 2 million people lived in Tokyo in 1923. Twenty times that number lived there when the 3rd quake struck. Around 5 percent of the population perished, nearly 2 million people. The population of Tokyo in 1923, gone in the 3rd Great Kanto Earthquake. I was in Kanda when it happened, surrounded by rubble. I don't like to remember it.

"Fine. But how does any of this help me?" I asked.

"It doesn't. But it keeps the police working on the case and not chasing after you. People like CDI Jones are like the Tokyo crows. They look for the shiny object and are relentless. I'm making sure that you, Mr. Lejeune, are not the shiny object." Konno said, and it made sense.

"Still, having the autopsy report would have helped. I couldn't even go to the combini this morning. Rumors about 'The Zach Tragic Murder House' are circulating in town. Whenever I go out, people stop talking as soon as they see me. The silence is unbearable." I said, running my hand through my hair. I missed my morning roasted tea. I couldn't even bring myself to buy a few inari to take the edge off my morning hunger.

"You couldn't go to the store because people weren't talking about you? That seems peculiar, Mr. Lejeune." My lawyer said.

"It does, doesn't it? It is simple. When the people around you suddenly stop talking, it means that before you arrived, they were talking about you. I am used to people whispering about me, but this? This is unbearable." I tried to make sense of it for Konno. I probably failed.

"Naruhodo." My lawyer said.

"Quite. I am glad you understand. Now, did you bring anything to eat? I am starving and have no desire to attempt the combini again." I smiled. Konno had arrived with little more than her OL special suit and a disposable briefcase.

"As a matter of fact, I do. Fukusawa-san gave me something for you. I met her coming up the steps. Here." Konno took a container out of her disposable and pushed it across my desk. Two onigiri and some rolled omelet. Very welcome. I had stopped keeping onigiri in my office after Saito had poisoned one of my former clients with a tainted rice ball.

I looked up from the food as someone knocked on my door.

"Expecting anyone else?" Konno asked.

"No," I answered, "Come in?"

Miki opened the door and entered. I wasn't expecting to see her today.

"Miki? What brings you here? Everything ok at Rufus'?" I asked.

"Zach. It's your place now, you should just accept it." Miki said as she pulled up a chair and sat down.

"Your manager is correct, you know. I delivered the papers to you myself." My lawyer added, not helping me at all.

"Don't remind me," I said, "What's up, Miki?"

"Since we found that body, there have been some odd rumors around Toranomon Downs. I ignored it at first, but then the rumors started getting strangely specific about the body. And you, Zach." Miki was calm, but I could tell the whole situation bothered her. Finding a decades old corpse in your place of business can do that.

"What sort of rumors? About me?" I asked.

"At first it was just that we found a body in the building. Yesterday, however, I started hearing that it was a body from the fire at Toranomon 41 a few months ago. The one while you were troubleshooting the new VR systems for Rufus. So I asked some questions." Miki told her story, and I listened.

"The more I asked around, the more the details came back to how you were inspecting the new systems when the fire broke out. A lot of talk about you being bad luck and a few people talking about how it isn't bad luck at all. How you must have been in league with your lawyer." Miki continued. My lawyer was sitting on the edge of her seat, listening. Miki stopped talking.

"And?" I prompted. My lawyer's heels were off the ground, her toes tipped forward waiting for Miki to speak.

"Wakabayashi. He spread the rumors." Miki said.

"Oh. And what do you want me to do about it?" I asked. Miki must have had something in mind.

"I want you to talk to him. I can deal with the rumors, but I can't deal with that NEET. I see red whenever he opens his mouth. Pleasant voice, but I still want to smash his face in." Miki looked down, ashamed of how much she disliked our lead technician.

"Alight. Can't we just fire him?" I asked.

"I wouldn't advise that, Mr. Lejeune. I think you should talk to him first. You need a solid basis, not just hearsay." Konno said.

"I agree, counselor. Thank you." I said. Konno was right, we needed more than just rumors. Rash action in the face of rumors just makes a situation worse.

"Miki, shall we go to talk to Mr. Wakabayashi?" I asked.

"Can I hit him?"

"No." My lawyer and I said together.

"Fine." Miki got up and led the way out of the office. All three of us headed towards Toranomon 41, home of 'The Zach Tragic Experience.'

We arrived about fifteen minutes later and started looking for Wakabayashi. We found him in the basement, examining the damage to the room where we had found the body. I honestly didn't remember much about the space. It was dark and there had been a horribly burned corpse in the room that had absorbed everyone's attention.

Now, without the body and with the electricity restored to the room, it was quite a different scene. Wakabayashi was surveying the scattered equipment and marking down his notes on a clipboard.

"Mr. Lejeune, I didn't expect you here today. How can I help you?" Wakabayashi said without looking higher than my knees.

I looked around at the damage. The room had been the scene of a fire, not a few months ago as in the rumors, but 17 years earlier. Electronic equipment, cables, and unidentifiable burned devices were squirreled into every corner of the room.

"Wakabayashi-san, what is all this?" I asked, distracted from the reason we had come. I could sense something was not right.

"Garbage. Although once this was state-of-the-art lab equipment. That over there? Multi-spectrum analyzer. Pre-Drift. I only ever read about them. This over here? No idea." Wakabayashi poked his pen into a burned out plastic and metal box. The place his pen touched collapsed from the slight pressure he exerted on it.

My lawyer was not amused and I could sense Miki

getting angry at me for not confronting the lead technician. I was about to say something when a loud metallic slap came from the hallway. We all turned to look at the middle-aged woman standing in the doorway pointing a shotgun in our direction.

"Matsumoto-san? When did you trade the flowers for that, what is it? A shotgun?" I asked.

"It's a VEPR-12, and you just couldn't leave well enough alone, could you?" the florist said.

"That's Russian," My lawyer said, "Magazine fed, semi-automatic ВПО-205, if I'm not mistaken?"

"Quite right. Now, all of you get in the far corner of the room." Matsumoto-san said, hefting the heavy-looking firearm. She had folded the stock forward and was keeping the barrel pointed in our direction. A short, stubby magazine extended just below the frame of the weapon. It could have held 4 or 5 shells at the most. Enough to deal with our small group.

"Now, tell me, why did you open my brother's tomb?"

THE GUN, THE EXPERIMENT, AND THE SACRIFICE

"Where did you get that gun, Matsumoto-sama?" My lawyer asked as Matsumoto herded into the corner of the burned lab in the basement.

"Shut up and sit down." Matsumoto, the florist said. She was a neighborhood feature in Toranomon Downs and the surrounding towns. Matsumoto-san always had the best flowers. Never a hint of gun oil.

"I am not comfortable with this, this situation." Wakabayashi said as he frantically looked at everyone's feet except Matsumoto's.

"Get a grip on yourself, Wakabayashi." Miki hissed at the lead technician.

"Did you restore all the power to this room, Wakabayashi?" Matsumoto demanded.

"Answer me."

"Yes." Wakabayashi said.

"Good. Now, who did this?" Matsumoto swung the barrel of the gun from one side to the other, sweeping us all in its path.

"Was that from the Russian Embassy? Before they abandoned Tokyo?" I asked.

"Yes. Now shut up." Matsumoto said.

"Oh, sorry," I said, "I just noticed that you seem to have kept it very well maintained. I mean, for a florist."

"I wasn't always a florist." Matsumoto said. My lawyer picked up on my lead.

"What did you say about the poor man who died here? He was your brother?" Konno asked.

"Yes. My brother. My dear, sweet Chiaki-kun." Matsumoto's eyes creased as she spoke her brother's name. There was a wetness that hadn't been there before. She loved her brother, dead these last 17 years.

"Matsumoto Chiaki. That is a wonderful name," I said, "He had an awful lot of hardware installed, didn't he? Was everything all right?"

"Ha. You know nothing. He was fine. Better than fine. It was all for the experiments." Matsumoto's eyes glimmered. She was excited by whatever these experiments were. Good excitement or bad, I couldn't tell.

"Is that why this building was so well shielded?" Wakabayashi asked. Curiosity must have won over his panic.

"That's a secret. Now you shut up, sniveling weasel. See that knob on the wall? Press it, or I'll start in with this." Matsumoto gestured at Wakabayashi with the gun. She meant what she said. Wakabayashi touched the soot-covered knob on the wall. It depressed, and a panel receded, drawing itself back and sliding to the right, disappearing into the wall. Secret pocket door. Fascinating.

A light flickered on in the newly revealed room.

"Get in." Matsumoto ordered.

"How?" I asked.

"What do you mean? Walk."

"No, how did he die? What happened to your brother, Chiaki-sama?" I clarified. Sometimes you can get people to talk by being vague. It draws them in and everyone likes to hear themselves talk. We needed time. I knew if we went into the hidden room, none of us would come out alive. Even with my talent, I was not sure luck would be on our side.

My talent is fickle. I can't make things happen. Statistically, I break the laws of random chance. Anything that might break, or can break, usually does when I'm around. I did the math once. I shift probability by at least 3 standard deviations. That means normally rare occurrences happen much more frequently when I'm around. For example, there was a chance that the shells in Matsumoto's shotgun could misfire or the cordite could have gone bad.

A 0.01 percent chance of that happening might be a 1 percent or even a 5 percent chance with me around. I sink bad luck. Murphy's law is my constant companion, and it is how I make my living. Unfortunately, it is also uncontrollable, and I wasn't about to bet my life, or anyone's life on a 5 percent chance of a misfire.

"The Drift. It fried our equipment in the middle of the experiment." Matsumoto said. She looked away from me as she remembered what happened that day.

"The probes caught fire. Chiaki-kun's head was so beautiful, ringed in yellows and blues. Flickers of green as the copper was immolated. As Chiaki-kun screamed." Tears were running down Matsumoto-san's cheeks. She loved her brother. Or the experiment, whatever it was.

"She's a psychopath." I heard Miki mutter. Unfortunately, so did Matsumoto.

"What did you say, you thick, steroid riddled thug? My

Chiaki-kun was beautiful. He exceeded every parameter. He could see everything in that moment. I watched him become a god, then the Drift took him from me. Shut your mouth, you muscle bound cretin. Better yet, let me." Matsumoto raised the shotgun, and my lawyer moved faster that I could think.

Her leg shot out and hit the barrel of the weapon. I thought I heard a click, but the gun didn't go off. Next, Konno-san rounded on Matsumoto and her other leg swung up and around, hitting the florist in the face and knocking her down. The gun clattered to the floor by the multi-spectrum analyzer.

"Miki, get the police." I yelled. Miki was a fighter, but Wakabayashi was an extreme introvert. I had to go with the person most likely to do what I said. Miki ran to the door, hesitated and looked back as my lawyer closed on the florist and assaulted her with a flurry of punches. The next moment, Miki was gone, running to get the police.

I turned to the two women fighting. It surprised me to see that the florist, the normally demure Ms. Matsumoto, was holding her own against my lawyer. I am not sure why the women in my life all know how to fight, but I wasn't about to question my good luck. I stayed back and kept Wakabayashi behind me.

"Why don't you just settle down and let me punch you?" Konno-san was saying. Matsumoto countered her strikes easily. She was right, she wasn't always just a florist.

"You broke into my brother's tomb. You need to pay. I kept this place secret. Safe. Then you and your Zach Tragic came along. Nakajima knew to leave well enough alone." Matsumoto said.

Rufus must have known about the body, or at least about the room. Nakajima was his surname, and he owned the building for years. Matsumoto must have had a deal with him.

"Why didn't you give him a proper funeral?" I asked, trying to get more out of the enraged sister.

"He was safe here. We worked so hard, he never would have wanted to leave. He saw the future. He knew." Matsumoto said as she raised her knee and kicked my lawyer in the stomach. Konno fell back. There was a lot of anger in Matsumoto's kick.

I didn't think, I just acted. I went to Konno's side and tried to help her up.

"Idiot." My lawyer scolded.

"Counselor, really?" I didn't pay attention when I should have. Matsumoto grabbed the gun from the floor and leveled it in our direction.

"Now you will all pay, starting with you, weasel." Matsumoto screamed. I moved. I jumped in front of Wakabayashi just as Matsumoto pulled the trigger. Click.

Click. Click. Nothing happened. It wasn't my talent. I can tell when probabilities shift and this wasn't what caused the shotgun not to fire.

"That's a 03 model, lady," My lawyer said as she got up and stepped in front of Matsumoto, "The ВПО-205-03, export model."

Konno grabbed the shotgun and ripped it from Matsumoto's grip. Matsumoto just stared. It was too much. Her brother's tomb, the shotgun not working, getting pummeled by my lawyer. It was all too much. She was in emotional shock.

"The 03 doesn't fire with the stock folded. Moron." My lawyer said as steps sounded on the stairs. CDI Jones, Officer Kato, and Miki came around the doorway. Jones had his revolver drawn.

Konno Asuka dropped the magazine out of the weapon, racked the bolt and ejected the shell from the chamber. She didn't smile.

"Here. Make yourself useful." My lawyer said to CDI Jones, handing him the shotgun.

Yes. Sometimes I think I love my lawyer.

"Mr. Lejeune. I am billing you double for today."

Yes. Sometimes I think I hate my lawyer.

4

TRAGIC AND THE SURVIVOR

THE INVITATION, THE JOB, AND THE ATTACK

I don't really understand how to run a business. That much had become clear to me over the past few months. Or maybe it was just my talent for breaking things? I shook my head as I read over the financial statements Miki had left for my review.

I did an acceptable job with my principal business, but I honestly understood nothing about running the *Zach Tragic Experience*. Miki, my sysadmin and operations manager, made sure I was aware of my failings on a daily basis. Not like I ever wanted to run a virtual experience salon.

"Fukusawa-san, why is this so hard to read?" I asked my landlady. Fukusawa had come over when she sensed my distress at having a spreadsheet in front of my eyes. That was my story, and I was sticking to it.

"I assume because you are a moron. But what do I know?" Fukusawa said as she stared at the numbers on the spreadsheet.

"Ha-ha. My job isn't accounting, it's finding problems. I get hired, I find problems, write a report, and get paid.

There are far too many entries on this, what is it called?" I looked up at Fukusawa, hoping for sympathy.

"Profit and loss statement. And this one is for expenses. And this one, well, this one is something I've never seen before." Fukusawa held up the paper for me to examine.

"Capitalization? I don't even know what those kanji mean." I said.

"It's the monetary investment in concrete things your business owns, Zach-chan. Like property, machines, and goods." A familiar voice said from my open door. Although open was not accurate, it was an open doorway, no door. Miki and her fellow employees had busted down my door when they tried to kill me. After that, and an encounter with a terrible but well-dressed lawyer, I hired Miki.

My lawyer was occupying the space where the door should have been. Behind her, I saw a familiar face. Matsumoto Reiko.

"Konno-san, Matsumoto-san, to what do I owe this pleasure?" I asked.

"A job. Or so I thought. Now I am having my doubts." Konno Asuka said as she walked up to my desk.

"Oh? Why is that?" I feigned disinterest. Matsumoto was one of my best clients and it was important she didn't think I knew that.

"How are you still in business, Mr. Lejeune?" Konno said, "These are basic financial documents."

"I don't usually deal with all this. I don't have a product, I consult. Like you. Like a lawyer, but more respectable." I tried a verbal jab with Konno. I knew I didn't stand a chance, but at the time I thought it was fun.

"I think you have mistaken respectable for disreputable. You're choice in lawyers has shown that to be true in the past, and it will probably be true in the future if I leave you to your own devices." Konno didn't mince words. She knew about my previous encounters with lawyers and she did not approve.

"But Konno-san, you are my lawyer." I said.

"Yes, but I chose you as a client, you did not have any input. It's better that way."

"Naruhodo."

"Well, delightful as this is, and it is always delightful to see you, Ms. Konno, I must be on my way. Do take care of my tenant, won't you, Konno-san?" Fukusawa stood and left the office, nodding to my lawyer and my client as she left.

"Now, on to business." Konno said, sitting in the better of the two chairs on the client side of my desk.

"As long as it doesn't involve spreadsheets." I said.

"It doesn't, but I'm still concerned. Lejeune-san. Zach. Are you ok? You seem out of sorts." Konno stated, probably for Matsumoto's benefit. My lawyer was exceptionally good. She was probably trying to up my fee using sympathy.

"I am fine, counselor. Miki's a delight to work with and she has all the financial details under control. I just wanted to take an interest in the regular operations." I said truthfully.

"Oh, Zach-chan? Are you interested in the regular operations of your skinless brothel?" Konno was teasing me. One of my former clients owned the *Zach Tragic Experience* before I did. My former lawyer poisoned my former client. I ended up being the lucky beneficiary of my client's untimely death. I didn't feel lucky looking at the spreadsheet. I needed to change the subject before the teasing became unbearable.

"Tell me about this job?" I looked at Matsumoto in anticipation.

"I am afraid this is a sensitive job. It requires discretion.

Can you handle that, Zach-chan?" Konno spoke. Matsumoto stood, not looking at me. Matsumoto Reiko was the best horologist in Tokyo. Probably the best in the world. Clockwork mechanisms had become critically important in Forgotten Tokyo. The failure of microprocessors after the Drift gave clockworks a new lease on life. I was not used to her acting demure.

"I need a date." Matsumoto said under her breath.

"What?" I was shocked.

"Omiai." Matsumoto said.

"I think you already know my answer." I said.

"Mr. Lejeune. Zach. I need you to put aside your personal feelings for a moment." My lawyer said.

"You know I do not have those feelings, counselor. What's going on?" I asked.

"My family tricked me." Matsumoto said, "They are setting me up for a vacation and an omiai."

"An omiai? What is this, restarting the feudal age? Since when does a family set you up for a marriage match-making?" I couldn't believe it. It had to be a trick.

"It's real. I checked. Matsumoto-sama has been right and properly set up and cornered. She must attend the family vacation and the family has arranged for a suitor from Kyushu to be present. All signs point to an omiai. Matsumoto-san knows you have no romantic feelings. She says she only feels safe with you, Zach-chan." Konno explained.

"I can't. I need to figure out this accounting. I have two businesses to run. Miki wants me to look this over." I made as many excuses as I dared. There was no way I was going to get my way with Konno and Matsumoto both in the room. I had as much chance as a kamakiri had of murdering a steamroller.

"I will send my accountants over to work your books. Zach, please?" Matsumoto said, looking down at me through her eyelashes. I almost felt a pang of something, but I'm just not built that way. However, I know the value of an accountant from the Yokoso Fruit company, however. That offer was worth its weight in gold, maybe the weight of the steamroller about to squash the mantis. If I was the kamakiri and the two women were the steamroller, then this mantis was ready to be flattened if Yokoso Fruits' accountants would get my books in order.

"Fine. When do we leave and where are we going?"

"Now. Here are your tickets." Konno said, pulling two train tickets out of the inner pocket of her Office Lady special suit jacket.

"Fujiisan. There's a lovely onsen at Narusawa." Matsumoto said. I stood up and pulled my jacket on over my vest.

"Then we should best get going." I said and headed to the door. I wish I had made it to the train, but I barely made it to the street.

"Well, Zakurai. Move and I'll cut you." An unfamiliar voice said as a familiar sensation pressed into my ribs. I don't know when the feeling of a knife point became familiar to me, but you can usually tell when someone means to use it by the pressure and steadiness of their prodding. The man was serious and would use the blade if he had no other choice.

"Who the hell are you?" My lawyer said from the stairs. Konno and Matsumoto had followed me down just as the unfamiliar man stepped beside me.

"Shut the hell up, I'm taking this dirt bag with me. Stay back or I'll stick him." The unfamiliar voice cracked slightly. Young and only a little desperate.

"He's got a knife. He'll use it." I said as I slowly raised my hands, "How can I help you, Mister?"

"You can't. Shut up, Zakurai." He looped a plastic zip tie around my raised wrist and used it to pull my arm back roughly. He connected a second loop to the first, and it found its way around my other wrist in short order.

"What's going on?" Matsumoto asked, peeking over my lawyer's shoulder.

"Go back to the office, Matsumoto-sama, I will handle this." My lawyer said. She was a rental lawyer, but she was the best. She was also skilled in hand-to-hand combat. I didn't know they taught that at law school.

The car that drove up suddenly was a surprise. A second surprise was my face getting an intimate introduction to the carpet in the car trunk. It smelled old and like oil. Diesel. Maybe a Merc or some other German car. Then it was dark. Surprise number three. I've been abducted before. It isn't fun or something you get used to happening. I hoped my lawyer was busy kicking the unfamiliar voice's butt.

As the car squealed its tires and drove away, I knew my lawyer had failed me. I twisted my wrists. My talent manifested. I heard a clicking as I worked the plastic zip ties. I may sink bad luck around me, but it can take effort for objects to fail. I hoped that by working the plastic back and forth, the small catch that locked the ratchet teeth on the zip ties would fail. Five minutes later, it did.

My wrists were free, but I was still locked in a dark trunk. Lucky for me, I could feel my talent surging. I'm a corollary to Murphy's Law. Everything that can go wrong, will go wrong. Usually when I'm around. That's the corollary. Thinks break in my vicinity. I kicked at the trunk and the lock gave way. The light was bright, and I took my chances. My talent doesn't affect me, but that doesn't mean bad things don't happen to me. I rolled out of the trunk and hit the pavement as the car sped away. It hurt like hell. I ran before my abductor could stop and catch me.

THE TELEPHONE, THE CLUE, AND
THE BLACKOUT

"COUNSELOR, I NEED YOU TO GET SOMEONE TO ME. I think I'm in in Kyobashi, I can see a sign for the Edo Momiji Dori. Whoever that was, they will notice I popped the trunk to get away. I'm gonna keep running. Check the metro stations. Call the police." I never call the police. Abductions are an exception. People willing to snatch you off the street and stuff you into a car trunk are dangerous. Cars are rare on the roads of Forgotten Tokyo. A diesel? Bone fuel car? It had to be ancient. You would think it would be easy to find, and it would be *if* you were the police. Until they got on the case however, getting abducted in an old, diesel bone fuel car made me concerned for my welfare.

I didn't know the voice. Usually the people that wish me harm are familiar. I didn't know the car. People who have cars have means or did, once upon a time. An unknown person of means that wished harm? I would need more than a rental lawyer to take care of this situation. Even my lawyer wasn't that good, and Konno Asuka was very good.

"Find me." I hung up the pay phone. Pay phones never

left Tokyo, but they made a big comeback when mobiles were no longer viable. The phone rang as I turned to exit the booth. Some awful gray-brown color tinted the giant cylinder's glass wall, ensuring privacy while letting others see when the booth was occupied. I picked up the receiver.

"Lejeune-san, is that you?" It was my lawyer.

"That was fast, are you ok?" I asked. Konno had my client to worry about when I got jumped. Hopefully Reiko was safe. Hopefully Konno kicked the morons in the teeth.

"Fine. I charge extra for personal defense. Triple if I get touched. Do you agree?" Konno was talking business. Never a good sign.

"Konno-san, this isn't the time. I agree, you're my bengoshi, counselor. Tell me you have someone to send to pick me up?" Triple was a high rate, but my lawyer was also an expert at close combat. I don't know where she picked up that skill, but it made her worth twice her weight in gold.

"You need to get somewhere public. Fast. Do you see any landmarks?" Konno was about her business. I could hear her writing on paper in the background. Passing instructions to someone, no doubt. Or tallying her fees.

"I don't see much. Low-rise buildings, not much traffic. Might be near where Tsukiji fell into the bay?" I was guessing, but I could smell the salt sea water, so maybe I was right.

"Find a metro. Or a JR Rail station. Call me when you get there. Now run, Zachie, run but keep your eyes open. Daruma-style. Ok, client?" Konno started calling me 'client' a month ago when she tried to get me to stop calling her counselor. It didn't work out as planned.

"Yes, counselor. On my way." I hung up and stepped out of the booth. I let the door close while I looked for a sign, a metro station, anything really.

The street was smaller, one or two tributaries off the main road, probably Edo Momiji Dori. I picked a direction perpendicular to the route the diesel had been heading and away from the smell of salty sea air. I had no intension of swimming away from my abductors.

I came to Heisei Dori and realized I wasn't where I thought I was in the city. I looked off to my right and there it was, the old Tsukiji Elementary School. I was a lot further south of Kyobashi and maybe a dozen blocks east of Edo Momiji. I was right where the sea air had hinted. Collapsed Tsukiji. The market the fish took back for their own.

My father had heard from his father about the old Tsukiji fish market. I had even seen a documentary on it once when I was in chu-gakou. The famous fish auction market. The whole place was legendary. Tsukiji had closed before the failed summer Olympics and the plague years, but that was long before I was born. Yet in the 7 or 8 decades since Tsukiji closed, it was still a legend. Even after the Tokyo Bay had reclaimed most of the land Tsukiji rested on during the 3rd Great Kanto Earthquake. Fish got their revenge, I guess.

The Higashi-Ginza metro station would be a few blocks west. I started a slow, loping run. I didn't want to attract too much attention. The streets weren't teeming with people, that wouldn't happen for another couple hours, but there were enough Tokyoites about their business that attracting attention might also draw my abductor's attention if they had doubled back to find me.

I should have run. I wouldn't have heard the diesel. I wouldn't have looked if I had run full speed to the metro. Instead, I heard the throaty growl of the engine. I turned and looked down the road and saw the car. I saw the driver, and he saw me. I didn't know who he was, but now I had a face to go with the unfamiliar voice. Unfortunately, I didn't realize he was a distraction. Everything went black.

I found out later that the driver had hired some tough guys who didn't ask questions as his muscle. Bouncers or nonsense like that. One of them smacked me across the back of my head with a bag of hundred yen coins. I hit the ground on my hands and knees, and the tough guy bagged my head in a big cloth sack. I couldn't see anything through the thick layers of the sack. My head was swimming and I couldn't focus my eyes.

'Concussion.' I thought to myself. After that, I tried not thinking because of the excessive pain that came along for the ride.

I didn't get dumped back into the trunk. The tough guy took one of my wrists in his hand and grabbed the back of the sack. I got pushed into the car, probably the back seat. A little luxury was all my escape bought me. Wonderful.

"You can't get away from me that easily, Tragic. Or would you rather be called the hero of Skytree? Nogitsune? Pick one, I don't give a damn. And after I make you pay, neither will you." The unfamiliar voice had a practiced speech. I needed to get a better, higher quality of haters. At this rate, I expected to hear 'No Mr. Lejeune, I expect you to die.'

Still, why Skytree? Skytree was seventeen years in the past. No one cared about me and what happened back then. The Drift was all anyone cared about from that time, anymore. Except this unknown voice. He cared. Cared enough to call me by both my nicknames. The hero of Skytree. In my opinion, I wasn't much of a hero. Apparently not in his either.

The Nogitsune of Skytree. A wild, magical fox. Might be good, might be bad. You never knew with a nogitsune.

Kitsune were uniformly good spirits. Hundred-year-old foxes who knew the secrets of magic and had wisdom to burn. Nogitsune were not Kitsune. Skytree was a tragedy with a thin silver lining of hope. My actions led to that hope and saving the lives of all of us trapped at Skytree on that day so long ago. Nogitsune it was. Tragedy masked with a thin veneer of hope. A wild fox, sometimes good, often bad. That was the real me, the actual hero of Skytree.

"What do you want?" I choked out. It hurt to speak. I had to figure out what the unfamiliar voice wanted from me.

"You'll find out soon enough. Ken, shut the fox up. I don't want to hear Zakurai's voice until uncle arrives." The unfamiliar voice said.

I heard the power outage sirens as the tough guy clapped a hand over my face. I could smell something through the sack. His hand had something in it, a sedative or something. Ether was a bit too cliché, but why not? Everything about today was a bit too cliché.

"How long until we get there, Sakata-san?" The tough guy was speaking. I had a name to go with the voice. And the face.

"Don't say my name." The unfamiliar voice scolded.

"It's fine. This scarecrow will be unconscious fast. I used double the dose on the rag." Great, the tough guy would probably kill me with the ether or whatever it was by accident. Not my preferred method of expiration.

"Don't kill him, you fool. I need him alive or this is all for nothing." Sakata said. I had a name to go with the voice now, if only I could stay conscious long enough to get more.

I didn't.

THE HANDCUFFS, THE ESCAPE, AND THE ZAPPER

I woke up in the dark.

"Naruhodo."

I was not amused and my head hurt from whatever drugs the tough guy put under my nose. Lovely. I hadn't had a migraine in years.

I sat in the dark and licked my lips. There was a dryness to the skin. The stiffness in my limbs told me I had been sitting for a while. I tested my arms, my legs. Everything felt in place. My wrists ached and were cold. Ah yes, handcuffs. I remembered the feeling. I wore a variety of them when I was young and popular. Mostly on the net drama, *Kudo's Repose*. At the time I didn't think much of it, but now I think the director was a fetishist.

I wasn't gagged, but I was secure in the chair. My arms pushed against the stiles of the chair on the inside of the back. I felt splats against my back. It was some western style wooden chair. As long as I wore the handcuffs, I wasn't going anywhere.

"Naruhodo."

I sat. I waited. I couldn't see. I was inside then, in a

room without windows. My eyes had enough time to adjust, and I still saw nothing but darkness. I pulled my hands apart. The handcuffs didn't let me move very far. Hinge link type, not a chain link. I wouldn't be able to twist my wrists or bind the chain. There would only be a couple links forming the hinge, making it hard to find a weakness in the construction. The hinge type cost more, but it's worth it for quality construction. I'm usually a fan of quality construction, but I made an exception in this instance.

"Naruhodo."

"Will you stop saying that? I find it annoying." It was Sakata. I wasn't alone.

"Sakata-san, I think your partner said? Hajimaemashite. Not really, but I don't want to be rude." I said, turning my head towards Sakata's voice.

"There will be time enough for that later, Zakurai. Tell me, is that really your name? Not a proper Japanese name, is it? But then neither is Lejeune."

"My grandfather was French. We kept the name." I said. Keep Sakata talking.

"Ah, so a half-Japanese? You don't look it." Great, hopefully Sakata wasn't one of those blood nationalist fanatics. Ignorant and annoying.

"Wrong. My grandfather was French, grandmother was Japanese. So was my father and my mother. I would be an eighth French and the rest of me is all Nippon Ham." Nippon Ham was my favorite baseball team. I couldn't resist that joke whenever someone made a nonsense aspersion about my family tree. Surprising how often it used to happen when I was younger and more well known.

"Well, aren't you the funny comedian?" Sakata was sitting, I was sure of it because of how his voice carried. We were in some sort of large area, but his voice was coming at a level similar to my own. The echo off the walls, floor, and ceiling when he spoke matched mine. I wouldn't have been able to tell in a smaller or more crowded space.

"Glad you could make the show, Sakata-san." I continued our conversation.

"I want you to meet someone, Zakurai. Someone you should remember." There was menace in Sakata's voice. I could just hear it when he finished his sentences. It was like the slow pull of a knife blade as it cut through a slab of fatty tuna. I loved otoro, but if I was the fish, I didn't want to be around to become the sushi.

"I can't wait to shake her hand." I said.

"His hand. You won't get the chance though. Uncle is going to watch you die. Just like you watched him all those years ago." I heard Sakata stand. Chair legs scraped the floor. Metal on concrete. His footfalls echoed, and then a light from the door blinded me as it opened. The door closed and Sakata was gone.

"Naruhodo." I said.

A young, desperate, but composed enough man. Sakata had planned my abduction well. Even with a few problems, he still pulled it off. Apparently I meant something to him. Something to him and his uncle. I had never seen him before; I was sure of that. Everything was so confusing. Or was that the ether and my migraine?

A flicker of light played across the floor and stabbed at my eyes. The room wasn't just blank walls. A curtain was getting blown in the wind. I strained, looking for the patterns. Another flicker and I saw the windows. There were heavy tarpaulins draped over the windows - on the outside of the windows. Where ever I was being held, it was under construction or renovation. The tarpaulins covered the construction site from the prying eyes of the public.

Another breeze and I saw out the window. The room was high over the city. I saw the familiar line of the Sumida river, Asakusa in the distance. Crap. I needed to get out of there. It all made sense, now. I should have seen it sooner.

I felt my talent rise. With enough effort and desperation I could sometimes jump start a statistically improbably event. I needed a statistically improbable event right now. I pushed. The talent cooperated. Something about my talent prefers it when I'm not dead. I think *he* knew if I stayed in this room, in this place, I would be mortally deceased.

The handcuffs clicked. Maybe the spring that locked the ratchet failed. I didn't know, and I didn't care. Things break, especially around a living accident like me.

I wiggled my hand and flicked the single strand jaw of one cuff open. I slipped out of the chair with the cuff still hanging on my right wrist. Not a problem. I needed to get out before Sakata came back with his 'uncle,' whoever the hell that was.

The tarpaulins blew as the wind grew stronger. Light defined some parts of the room. I saw the door Sakata used. On the other side of the space was another door. A maintenance door. Six-hundred and forty plus meters is a long way to climb, but fortunately I knew I wasn't on one of the top floors of Skytree. I headed for the maintenance door, opened it and entered the stairwell to make good my escape.

The lights were on as I started loping down the stairwell. One step, two, occasionally three at a time. My body felt stiff and tingled with some slight loss of circulation. Small price to pay when life was on the line.

Down I went. Scattered tools littered the stairwell: hammers, toolboxes, and the occasional mop and bucket. I came to a landing and caught my breath. There a toolbox and a hammer. I picked up the hammer and opened the toolbox. I got lucky. There were a variety of screw-drivers in the box. I grabbed a thick one and placed it over the keyway of the handcuff still attached to my wrist. Holding it was awkward with one hand still locked in, but I managed and struck a blow on the end of the screwdriver. I struck three more blows and the lock mechanism shattered. I shed the cuffs and discarded the tools. On reflex, I thanked them for their service and hoped to never see them again in my natural or unnatural life.

I kept going down. I wasn't sure how high up I was in the structure of Skytree, but soon I came to another mainte-nance door. A mop and its bucket were leaning against it. I grabbed the mop and tried the door. It opened, and I squeezed tight against the wall. The room looked empty and was larger than the previous room. There were lights and a generator. More tools. The construction workers probably used it as a staging area. I stepped out, keeping the mop as a precaution. The area used to be one of the art galleries. If I remembered correctly, there was an elevator close by. Quick trip to the exit. Escape and find my lawyer. Charge her double for not rescuing me. A solid plan.

I hadn't been back to Skytree in almost 17 years. Not since the Drift. Not since myself and a dozen tourists almost died when everything modern stopped working as the magnetic pole of the planet split itself into five massive chunks of molten iron fighting each other for dominance deep in the planet's mantle.

Fun times. I stopped in front of the elevator and pressed the button. Wait. I hoped they had turned off the music. Wait. Ding. I faced the doors as they opened. It surprised me to see Sakata standing in the elevator with an old man in a wheelchair. I knew the man. I knew him very well when we were both younger.

"Ryusuke?" I said. I make big mistakes when I'm surprised. This mistake gave Sakata enough time to press a stun gun to my chest and electrify the fight out of me. I hate making big, dumb mistakes. Especially when accompanied by 40,000 volts and unconsciousness.

THE DRIFT, THE MOP, AND THE MYSTERY

"Zakurai, wake up. It's almost time for your encore." Sakata said.

"Nephew, why are you doing this?" Ryusuke was speaking. That was unusual. Ryusuke's injuries made it hard to speak.

"Not now, uncle. I'm busy with preparations." Sakata said.

Everything felt off. My teeth, my breathing. Everything.

"I hope that isn't too tight, Zakurai. No, actually, I do. Scream a little so I know when not to stop?" Sakata seemed a little too happy about whatever he was doing to me. Honestly, I was still unclear what was going on. Getting a 40,000 volt potential discharged into your chest will do that even if the amperage is too low to kill. Probably why it's called a stun gun and not an electro-killer, or something equally imaginative.

"Ryusuke-san, nice to see you again. How long has it been? Five years? Ten?" I asked, trying to get a look at the surrounding room.

Sakata had trussed up. Clearly, he was a fetishist. Why

would Ryusuke's nephew would fixate on me, however? That was a mystery. I moved my shoulders to work out the stiffness. I started swinging. Great. Sakata had me trussed up and lifted off the floor.

"Tell me, Sakata-san, is there a reason I'm blindfolded?" I felt the constriction around my arms and legs. I guessed he had me bound with ropes or maybe tie-downs of some sort.

"Well, that's what it was like when the Drift started, wasn't it? The lights were out. Everything was dark. Isn't that right, uncle?" Sakata said as he strained at something. I guessed it was a rope attached to a pulley or a block and tackle of some sort as I started a slow, jerking rise in my bonds.

"Nephew, this is wrong." Ryusuke said, and then I understood. Skytree. The Drift. Ryusuke's injuries. And me.

"Yes, Sakata-san. The lights went out. We were all trapped. Me, the tourists, your uncle Ryusuke. What is it you want?" I asked.

"You bastard. You have to ask? You did this. You unmade the man my uncle was. You and your cursed bad luck." Sakata was oddly calm. Not quite rehearsed, but calm with a slight sharpness.

"My bad luck? I didn't have bad luck back then. Do you think what happened was because of me? I can assure you, Sakata-san, even now my bad luck isn't strong enough to split the magnetic load of the planet." Obviously, Sakata was confused. Back when the Drift occurred, I was just a normal net-drama star. A television talent. Maybe even a bit of a bishi-boy. I didn't gain my starring role in Murphy's Law until seven years later, at Kanda. Until *he* came into my life.

The Drift changed everything. Microprocessors were

no longer reliable after that day. Storms of charged parti-
cles occasionally burst through the planet's fractured
magnetosphere, frying electronics at random. Sometimes
powerful storms in the sun would send deadly waves of
matter at the planet, frying more than just electronics.
Civilization turned backwards on itself. We began using
old systems. Relays and switches instead of transistors and
chips. Computers were out, paper was in. The internet
and net-dramas were gone. Analogue televisions returned.
Mass communications failed, and with them, hubs of technology and connection died and were forgotten. Tokyo
was forgotten. People still knew we were there, we just
weren't as important anymore. Modern communications
had made Tokyo a hub of world culture, and overnight, it
was gone.

I had been here on the day it all happened. Ryusuke
was a guide at Skytree. He stood outside the elevators
greeting tourists and people like me. The lights went out
first. The Drift blew out power distribution throughout
Tokyo. Ryusuke kept everyone calm. We just needed to
wait for the power to return according to him.

Changes in the planet's magnetic field affected many
systems, including navigation systems. We didn't know that
planes would fall out of the sky. When the wing of a private
airplane clipped Skytree as its navigation system lost its
mind, we panicked. A sudden blast of noise and air tore
through Skytree as a great gash appeared in one wall while
we waited for the power to return. After that, no one was
going to wait for the power to return.

"Sakata-san, what are you going to do here?" I asked. I
thought I knew, but I wanted him to say it.

"It's simple. You dropped my uncle. I am going to drop
you." Sakata said.

"I dropped Ryusuke? Is that what you think happened?" I almost didn't believe my ears.

"Of course you did. The stunt of getting all those people out on the maintenance stairs? Even with the damage to the safety walls? Using the rope to give them confidence? Very clever. I'm sure it helped your reputation as a big star." Sakata had rehearsed this speech. Villain monologue time, I thought to myself.

"We were all panicking. There was a great gash in Skytree. I did what I thought would get everyone out, and it did." I said. No sense in trying to reason with him. Sakata had made up his mind.

"And pushing my uncle off the building? When did that become part of your plan?"

"Pushing me? Nephew, that isn't what happened." Ryusuke protested.

"Not now, uncle, the adults are talking." Contempt was in Sakata's voice. I felt the wrongness that accompanied my talent. I heard the twist and crackle in the rope. I braced myself as best as I could.

"You visited uncle Ryusuke for years. Every year. I listened to you talk to him. Talk about that day with him. Even when he was stuck in his chair, spine broken from the fall at Skytree. The rope ruined him, the rope you tied around his waist to keep him safe." The ropes around my waist gave slightly.

"I figured it out later, when I was older. Coming down the maintenance stairs, you felt the breaking of the structure beneath your feet. Your bad luck caused the metal fatigue in the beams. You pushed uncle to save yourself and the rope caught him short, snapping his spine! It's all your fault, Lejeune Zakurai!" Sakata had convinced himself of a story and there was no way to make him see the truth.

"No." Ryusuke said from his wheelchair, "I pushed Zach-sama. He saved us. I wanted him to live."

The rope snapped, and I rolled as I hit the floor. The bindings came loose. Sakata had used the rope to both bind me and pull me up in the air. He knew nothing about knots. I pulled the blindfold off and blinked my eyes to see. My hand was on the mop I had brought with me into the room. It would have to do.

I stood and put my foot on the mop head. I spun the handle, unscrewing it from the head. Holding the mop handle like a shinai, I stood at guard against Sakata.

"A mop?" Sakata said with disdain in his voice, "I've got a knife."

It was true, Sakata had a knife. Not that it mattered. He hefted it in his left hand and held the stun gun in his right hand. I closed on him with the mop handle held loose. Sakata smiled. He was confident. From my point of view, overconfident.

"Please, don't hurt him?" Ryusuke said, pleading.

"I think it's too late for that, uncle." Sakata made a move to attack.

I swung a tight circle to the left with the mop and Sakata predictably went the other way, thinking to avoid the strike. It was a feint, and I caught his wrist solidly. The knife flew out of Sakata's hand. A moment later, the stun gun hit the ground as I used the mop back swing to hit Sakata's other wrist. Double 'kote.' I was inside Sakata's guard, so I struck his chest on the left side and then the right. Sakata wasn't a fighter. He didn't have the training to react. Probably didn't know what hit him, so I scored a 'men' right on top of his head so he knew what hit him. Sakata went down hard.

"He wasn't talking to you, son." I said, "Ryusuke, are you ok?"

I collected the knife and the stun gun as I walked over to my old friend.

"I'm so sorry you got dragged into this, Ryusuke. Does it hurt?" I asked.

"It always hurts, Zach-sama. But I'll be alright. I'm so sorry for this. He was always such a dutiful child. Attentive. I didn't know he blamed you for my condition."

"It's ok, Ryusuke. Let's get you home." I said.

Just then my lawyer burst in through the main entrance door. She had some local Sumida police with her. They were dragging the tough guy who drugged me along, probably as a guide. I looked at them as they surrounded Ryusuke, Sakata, and myself.

"Good timing. How did you find us, counselor?" I asked.

"I got a call from you, client." Konno said.

"All the way back at Tsukiji? That's some fine detective work, counselor." I complimented my lawyer.

"No, the call you made after that. At Asakusa." Konno looked at me with a puzzled expression.

"I didn't call you from Asakusa. That moron had me in a car, then tied to a chair, then here." I pointed at Sakata, unconscious on the floor.

"Someone called me. Said it was you. Said the abductor was taking you to Skytree. I asked about a ransom, but then the phone cut off." Konno said.

"Well, then I guess we have a mystery friend, don't we?" I said, "By the way Konno-san, I charge double for rescuing myself."

"Sometimes I hate my clients." Konno said with a smile.

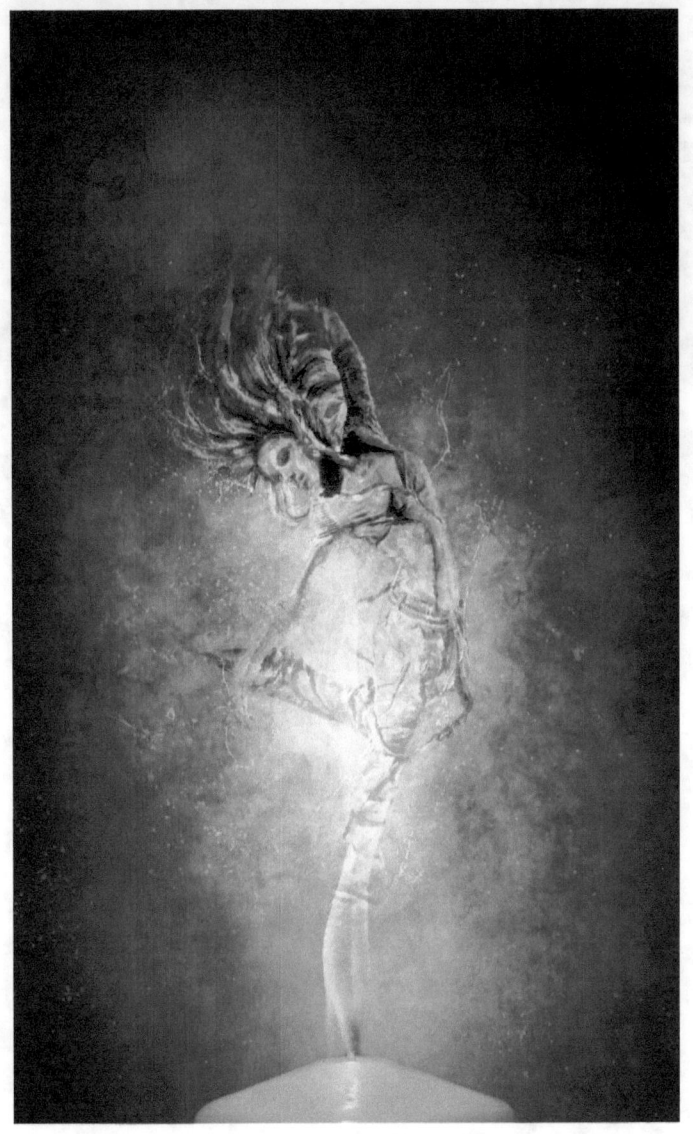

5

TRAGIC AND THE TARRASQUE

THE TRAIN, THE STOP, AND MAIHAMA

OBON COMES AND OBON GOES. I USUALLY HELPED MY mother wash the family graves in Chiba during obon. The trip to Chiba was lonely and boring. I took the JR-East train from Tokyo Eki, made some station changes, and ended up on the Keiyo Line headed for the countryside. Most years, I slept on the train. Sleeping helps, especially in the August heat.

This August, I didn't sleep. A few weeks before I had taken on a very special job for one of my best clients, Matsumoto Reiko. Matsumoto-sama is a genius of mechanical engineering. She made the machines that kept Forgotten Tokyo running. Reiko was brilliant, respected, and unmarried. Her family was only happy with two of those three conditions of her otherwise flawless existence.

Matsumoto-sama's family had set her up for an omiai - traditional match-making. Reiko, not being a feudal Japanese woman, was having none of it. Unfortunately, these things fester and come up over and over again unless put into a timely grave. Reiko hired me to do that just before the nephew of an old acquaintance abducted me. The nephew wanted revenge for an accident that happened a decade earlier. He wanted me dead. It didn't take.

After freeing myself from my abductor, Reiko insisted I fulfill my hired task and escort her to the unwanted omiai, nominally posing as her ne're-do-well boyfriend. Potential matrimonial bliss seemed to be slightly better than impending death, so I agreed. Reiko knows I don't have a girlfriend. She also knows the thought of a romantic relationship is something that doesn't happen in my brain. Reiko wanted me for precisely that reason. No chance of mixed messages or other shenanigans. Zach Tragic is a safe bet with matters of the heart and flesh.

The job was a roaring success. For Matsumoto Reiko. It was an abject disaster for Lejeune Zakurai. When I was young and tragically pretty, I was a net-drama star. Net-dramas were the rage before the Drift took away our computers. I was very much in demand for hard-bitten dramas, featuring impossibly pretty young men. Fortunately for me, my stardom died with the rise of the electromagnetic anomalies that plagued the planet after the magnetic core broke up into at least five distinct blobs of molten iron. The blobs drifted away from each other and set up a multipolar magnetosphere that wreaked havoc with modern electronics.

Unfortunately for me, Matsumoto Yuko, Reiko's mother, was a stalker-fan of net-dramas and of *Kudo's Repose* in particular. *Kudo's Repose* was the net-drama that made me a star. Matsumoto Yuko was absolutely smitten that her daughter was dating her favorite talento. So smitten that she tried to corner me in compromising positions at the onsen no less that five separate times. Twice while Reiko was watching. Reiko loved every minute of my discomfort. I don't know if I love or hate her for that. Probably both. We'll laugh about it next time we have a nomikai.

"Why do you let that bimbo sleep on you like that, Zach-kaicho?" Miki asked from her window seat next to me on the train.

"You don't let Matsumoto-sama do anything. She does what she wants." I said. Miki had planned on coming home with me during obon since she had no family of her own to visit. I found out about her plan two days earlier. I trusted Miki to make decisions for *The Zach Tragic Experience*, my unwanted virtual experience business, and apparently I trusted her to make decisions about my holidays as well.

"You could have said no." Miki was not fond of Reiko. I had no idea why.

"I tried. She made it awkward." I said, "Sometimes you just can't reject a kind offer."

Miki flexed her arms. She flexes when she's unhappy or frustrated. She was probably a little of both sitting on the train with me and Reiko. Built like a boxer, Miki was all fast-twitch muscles and mass. She scared me sometimes because she had the skill to back up the appearance. She was also a brilliant system administrator and ran the daily operations at the virtual experience parlor I had inherited from a murdered client. I had nothing to do with the murder. It was my bengoshi's fault. Until recently, I had poor taste in lawyers.

"Besides, after you informed me I was taking you home for obon, how could I say no to her?" I retorted. I didn't break a smile, although I desperately wanted to do just that.

"We are not equivalent. Don't even imply that I am anything like your bimbo client." Miki was clenching her jaw.

"I am implying nothing, Miki-san. I'm just amused that

for the first time, I'm bringing company home for obon. It is very irregular." I might have let a small smile out. Miki didn't hesitate to punch my shoulder. It hurt just enough.

"Are we there?" Reiko said sleepily.

"No, Matsumoto-chan. Go back to sleep." Miki spoke to her like a high school girlfriend. I winced.

"Yes, Miki-kun. I'll do that. Zach-chan, you're lumpy." Reiko said as she adjusted my shoulder to suit herself.

"Thanks. I don't know what I would do without you both keeping me occupied during obon." I looked longingly at my bag on the floor between my feet. I'd brought a book with me tucked away safely in my bag. Unread.

"Probably drink yourself stupid on the train." Miki said.

"And succumb to your employee's wicked plans." Reiko teased. Miki punched my shoulder.

"Ow! Why did you hit me?" I rubbed my sore shoulder.

"Target of opportunity. Besides, you squeal like a child. More satisfying." Miki looked me dead in the eyes. She meant it. Great. Was my operations manager a budding sadist? That would be an entirely unforeseen complication.

The lunch steward pushed his cart by us just then. Most long haul trains had vendors that moved through each car selling lunches and other treats to passengers. The shorter-run trains that left Tokyo had begun the service after the Drift made travel difficult. The steward was selling eki-ben. Special train station bentos were always popular. He had an excellent selection, but the aji looked best. I asked for an aji lunch box. Miki hit me in the shoulder again. I asked for two. Miki hit me a third time, and I asked for three. Definitely a sadist. Or possibly a very considerate person. I wasn't sure which.

"Reiko will want something to eat when she wakes up." Miki said as she stashed two of the eki-ben away in her bag for later. I put mine down on the fold out tray in front of me and opened it. Something about horse mackerel is tastier on a train. I think it's the naturally strong and oily fish. It recalls when trains were steam powered, mechanical monstrosities.

I paid the steward. He took my money and counted out my change. The train uniform looked tight on him and was probably second hand. Vendors often passed down their business to their children. Honestly, the uniform looked older than the steward. The only new item was the radio on his shoulder. He clicked the transmit button and spoke quietly into his radio. Calling ahead for more aji eki-ben, I supposed. Mackerel had always been very popular.

"You could have just told me to get two more. You didn't have to hit me again." I said.

"Not satisfying enough. Now you'll remember and become a better person." Miki smiled. Definitely enjoying my discomfort.

"Fine. But can we keep the injuries to a minimum from here on out?" I asked.

Miki didn't have time to answer as the train jerked, and a siren blared. It threw me forward into my eki-ben. Reiko fell forward off my shoulder as the emergency brakes engaged on each of the cars of the train. Miki braced herself against the seats in front of us. Her reflexes were fast, probably because she was a trained boxer.

"Why are we stopping?" Reiko asked.

"I don't know," I said, "But this isn't my talent. I think this is a genuine accident, or someone pulled the emergency stop." Miki and Reiko both knew about my talent. I'm a corollary to Murphy's Law. Anything that can go wrong, goes wrong when I'm around.

The public address system cracked, and a voice came

from the speakers. There was an apology, regrets, and other expressions of remorse for the untimely and unannounced stop. Apparently there was an obstruction on the tracks and the engineer was stopping the train. With luck, the delay would be minor, the voice said.

The train slowed, but stopping so much mass quickly was a fool's errand. I looked out the window to see where we would spend some time until they cleared the track. The peaks of an old luxury resort hotel were just coming into view. We must have been near Maihama. The old amusement park, some cartoon travesty of commercialism and animatronic novelty, perched to the right side of the rail line through the town of Maihama. Or rather, what remained of the town of Maihama. The Drift had destroyed most of the park's business with its heavy reliance on microprocessors and networked computers to keep all the rides safe. The power for the park alone had been tremendous. Now, it was mostly closed, and most of the town had closed along with the park's ill fortune.

A loud thud came from the front of the train. I jerked my head forward at the sound. The voice coming through the speakers let out a brief squeal and then a longer curse. The worker must have forgotten to un-key the microphone.

"That didn't sound good." Reiko sat bolt upright. She was fully awake and alert. Normally I don't worry about trains, but given a mechanical failure, I didn't think it bode well for our journey to my parent's home for grave tending during the obon holiday.

"What do you think it is?" Miki asked, her eye were wide. I thought something might have scared her.

"I'm not sure, but I think one car might have come off the tracks." Reiko speculated. I didn't know if that was true, but if the mechanical genius of the Yokoso Fruit company said the train derailed, then I was going with her intuition. I like safe bets.

"Shouldn't we be dead? Or falling into the sea or something?" Miki was scared. She was an excellent boxer and an even better system administrator, but she wasn't much of a mechanical engineer.

"We were braking, so our momentum was relatively low. You watch too many old net-dramas. Trains don't fly off the tracks." Reiko said.

"Unless you're me." I said, thinking of Kanda.

"Not helping, boss." Miki gritted her teeth.

"We should go see what's wrong." Reiko said.

"Oh, no." I knew what was coming.

"Can't the train people take care of it?" Miki asked.

"Not likely. They'll just call for help. Engineers are glorified forklift drivers. They need me." Reiko had a fire in her eyes. She had found something to fix.

Reiko was up and moving. I pulled out my pocket watch and checked the time. The watch was an old, mechanical wonder. It was self-winding and relied on nothing more modern than the nineteenth century. The clockworks in it had never failed me and never succumb to my talent. Anything that reliable was worth its weight in gold.

"Matsumoto-san, wait up. The train hasn't stopped yet." I called after her as I checked the time, again. Miki was getting up and following me.

We stopped at the door between the cars. The steward was on the floor, covered in eki-ben and blood. Reiko was just staring at him. As wonderful as Reiko was with machines, she was crap with people. The dazed steward had blood on his face. I bent down to look at him.

"Miki, grab a first aid kit, would you?" I asked as my employee tromped up behind me.

"Got it, boss. Let me in there, ok? I'll assist." Miki said as she pushed Reiko aside.

I reached for the steward's wrist and looked at the second hand on my watch. Find the pulse. Take a quick check and get the vitals. The pulse was there and strong. I didn't bother timing it. I reached into my vest for a penlight. I always carry basic tools. My business is finding problems. My talent for attracting misfortune helps me find those problems, but having the basic tools to do the legwork yourself never goes out of style.

I shined the light into the steward's eyes. I was looking for his pupils to respond. He jerked and grabbed my hand, sending my watch clattering to the deck of the car.

"Hey, calm down. You're fine." I said. The steward looked around rapidly with his eyes. He might have had a neck injury, so I gently took his hand and tried to relax him.

"So sorry. I think I hit my head. It hurts." The man said.

"You're ok. Where does it hurt?" I asked.

"I'm going to move forward, ok, Zach-chan?" Reiko said. She stared at the blood on the steward's face. If she didn't move forward, I would probably have a second patient to tend.

"Yeah, go ahead. We'll catch up." I said as Reiko nodded, opened the door, and moved into the next car.

"Girlfriend gone? Here's the kit." Miki said as she kneeled down beside me.

"Yeah. Reiko doesn't handle broken people very well. It's actually how we met." I said.

"Story later, I have some water and a cloth. Let's clean this guy up?" Miki was all business.

I took the wet cloth and started dabbing at the steward's

head. I wanted to blot the blood away and find the source of the fluids.

"So sorry. Here, you dropped this." The steward picked up my pocket watch and stuffed it into my vest pocket.

"Hey, that's fine. We need to see what's the matter with you. Don't worry about that, ok?" I tried calming the man again. He apparently didn't want to inconvenience me by making me look for my watch or bleed on my clothes. I found the wound. It was on the hairline of his scalp. There was a good amount of blood, but the cut was shallow and mostly clotted up already. Thank goodness for minor good fortune. I'm used to bad luck, so when good luck comes my way, I'm genuinely surprised.

"Boss, I got this. You should go forward in case your princess comes across any more injured people." Miki was right. I handed her the cloth and patted the steward on the shoulder before I got up and went after Reiko.

The front car was a mess. I could see it from the door. The car had derailed, and the front was significantly lower and tilting to the right. Reiko was arguing with a conductor or the engineer. I wasn't sure which, but by the time I got through the door and stood next to them, he was apologizing and bowing deeply to Reiko. She must have browbeaten him into submission. Usually Reiko's reputation as the horologist of Forgotten Tokyo makes people stand in awe of her. The man had been arguing with her, so he didn't know who she was. Reiko was the clockwork genius who had rebuilt much of the city to its former glory. The engineer, and he was the engineer as I could see from the pin on his uniform, was just now learning exactly with whom he was arguing.

I just watched. Apologies amuse me. So does seeing someone understand how outclassed they are by my client's intellect. I may not feel love and romance like other people, but it's hard not to feel something for the shear brainpower on Matsumoto Reiko.

"While I am sure that your explanation of why the train shouldn't be derailed and what this lovely man should have done better is interesting, Matsumoto-sama, why don't you let him call his supervisor?" I was interrupting the genius at work. The engineer needed the help.

"Oh. Right. Zach-chan, I think we can let this idiot fix the problem. Call your boss. Get the equipment I told you about out here. We have to get to Chiba for obon." Reiko concluded her argument and turned away from the man. I mouthed the words "go," to him, and he took the hint.

"Honestly, what was he thinking? And how does a bale of hay fall on the tracks from the one truck on the highway out here? In Maihama of all places?" Reiko spoke out loud.

"Hay bale?" I asked.

"Yes. It fell from the elevated highway next to the tracks. Right here is the only place for at least a kilometer where the road is above the train tracks. Now we have to get heavy cranes out here and not only clear the tracks, but pull this sorry train car off and replace it before we can continue down the line." Reiko started pacing and pointing with sharp jabs at the road, the hay bale, and the rails. She punctuated each problem with an offended jab.

"I guess that means the holiday is off?" I smiled. We could go back to Tokyo and I could ditch my client and my employee. I was sure there was still some umeshu at my office. I could send a letter with regrets to Chiba. Mom would understand.

Miki and the steward walked up behind us with her supporting the young man. An astonishingly small gauze

and tape bandage adhered to his forehead. He looked better, but still not fantastic.

"No way, Zach-kaicho. I didn't come all this way with her to be covered in some stranger's blood, not to have my holiday." Miki protested.

"What can we do? We're stranded on a train in the middle of some run-down suburbs. We could walk back to my office and get there before we reach my family home in Chiba. We don't even know anyone in Maihama. Where would be stay? No, we should wait for the railway to get us back to Tokyo." I said, confident in my logic.

"Well, I'm sorry we ruined your holiday," said the young steward, "but my grandfather is the caretaker for the old MiraCoast hotel at the park. He opens it for big holidays like obon."

"It's probably booked, or out of our price range." I felt my logic exhibit hairline fractures.

"Oh, no. It's a huge hotel, and he also manages the park." The steward said.

"It's not out of my price range." Reiko said unhelpfully. The fractures became fault lines.

"It would be a burden on your grandfather." I said, grasping at anything to halt the inevitable.

"He loves guests. I must insist. You should stay here, and I can talk Ojisan into giving you a tour of the old rides. He always runs a few of them during obon." said the steward. I could feel the light in Reiko's eyes and the fire of her curiosity at the thought of seeing the old rides and animatronics working again. The fractures turned to crumbling chasms lines of logic.

"Well, we could stay at the hotel. As long as we are here in Maihama, of all places. Tell me Zach-chan, how do you feel about staying in an old-school, high-end, luxury hotel with not one, but two beautiful and intelligence women? My treat." Reiko jabbed a finger at me. Apparently I had become a problem that needed a solution. Reiko would turn any logical argument against the plan into rubble and dust. The only solution to this problem was the old park, the hotel, and a few laughs at my expense.

THE HOTEL, THE PARK, AND THE BURNED BODY

THE STEWARD'S NAME WAS SANO AKI. REIKO HAD taken to calling him Aki-chan. Miki just referred to him as 'that Sano person.' I tried not to speak to him directly at all. I wanted this so-called vacation to be over, not turned into an extended stay at a former luxury hotel that I couldn't afford in its prime, and couldn't afford now, either.

"Guests used to come off the train and into a shopping area. It collapsed when the big quake struck and was never rebuilt." Aki-chan was going on about the big, open garden with nothing in it but plants. I didn't care.

"Naruhodo." I said.

"Fascinating, Aki-chan. Why wasn't the shopping center rebuilt?" Reiko asked our nearly adolescent guide.

"Grandfather said there was so much damage and loss of life when the quake happened that he would rather give the ghosts a nice place to relax. So he spent a year clearing the rubble and building the garden." Aki-chan explained.

"Naruhodo." I said. Miki hit my shoulder. I was getting numb from her constant assaults. I felt bad. I knew the 3rd Great Kanto Earthquake wasn't my fault. I was sure it wasn't Taira no Masakado's fault either. The kami that gave me my talent for misfortune was wrapped up in the disaster's history. Taira no Masakado was a rebel, an insurgent, finally a shogun. He was also a part-time resident in my head and the full-time source of my talent, causing Murphy's Law to go off the rails when I was nearby.

"Here is the entrance to the MiraCoast and the old sea park. Most of the water drained when the sea wall broke, but grandfather repaired that and refilled the lake." Aki-chan continued his tour-guide narrative. He must have worked for his grandfather and given the tour before he became a steward on the train.

The entrance was still grand. Old and weathered, but grand never- the-less. They designed the facade to look like a Tuscan village. Muted pastel colors adorned individual faux-Italian townhouses. The scene looked to be out of a fantasy from a few hundred years earlier. Here and there, cracks in the plaster showed the actual structure beneath the fantasy. Reinforced metal bars and fiberglass impregnated concrete peeked through where the fantasy and illusion failed to sustain itself. The amusement park was nearly a century old and honestly had seen better days, but knowing that only Aki-chan's grandfather and close family had maintained the entire 50 hectare site was astonishing. Even to me, mostly.

"Aki-chan, what are you doing here? I thought your train was more important than our family?" A very block-like old man called from one window of the MiraCoast hotel.

"I guess he's that Sano person's ojisan?" Miki whispered to me.

"Naruhodo." Miki hit my shoulder before I finished my word. The abuse felt familiar, like a ritual comfort.

"Grandfather, the train had an accident. I brought some passengers to stay for the weekend. Come see." Aki-chan yelled up to the old man. I could swear the whiskers on his mustache twitched at his grandson's words.

"Ojisan! I'm Matsumoto Reiko. Pleased to meet you!" Reiko shouted, positively bouncing with enthusiasm. My heart sank.

"Matsumoto the horologist?" The old man called back.

"The same! Have you heard of me?" Reiko was good at false modesty. It wasn't possible to live within 100 kilometers of Forgotten Tokyo and not have heard of Matsumoto the horologist.

"Aki-chan, you redeem yourself. Wait there while I come down." The old man called as he disappeared from the window and appeared at the entrance to the MiraCoast a scant five minutes later.

"Boy, bring your guests here to meet me." The old man called to Aki-chan. Reiko bounced over while Miki led me like a petulant child to exchange greetings with an abhorred relation. I put very little effort into our exchange of greetings. It earned me a punch from both Miki and Reiko. Now both shoulders hurt.

Sano Hideaki was the old man's name. He must have been in his eighties, but he was built like a barrel of sake. His bow was fluid and showed no signs of his age, but his eyes were foggy with early cataracts.

"Ojisan, do you take care of the entire hotel yourself?" Reiko asked.

"I do what I can, young lady. Do you take care of all the machines in Forgotten Tokyo?" The elder Sano replied.

"Of course not, but I think I see what you mean. Does Aki-chan help you?" Reiko continued their conversation while I tried to ignore it.

"I'll show you to your rooms while Ojisan entertains your companion." Aki-chan said, leading us into the MiraCoast.

The lobby was more than I had expected. A stone fountain with a series of fish and characters from the original cartoon attractions adorned the sculpted centerpiece. I wanted to hate it, but it was well crafted.

The adornments on the pillars and counters were gilt and aged. The original was artificially aged, but these details had the feel of real, earned longevity. Aki-chan stepped behind the mammoth counter that formed a semicircle around the wall on the far side of the fountain. I watched as he searched under the counter, moving from one end to the other. Sounds of opening boxes and sorting through what was likely random tools, hardware, and perhaps room keys accompanied his long progress down the counter. It felt rehearsed to me.

"Here it is! Not the best rooms in the hotel, but this is an especially delightful suite. I don't know if you are a couple or a family, but there are four separate bedrooms just in case you need options." Aki-chan explained as he rounded to far end of the counter and presented us with two card keys and two manual keys in case the electronic cards failed to work.

Radio frequency devices were increasingly rare because of the Drift. Passive devices like hotel key cards were fairly simple and harmless, but a surge in an electromagnetic field could overload the inductive coil and send a destructive spike of power into the integrated circuit buried in the plastic card. The manual keys were backups in case the cards were trashed.

"I'll leave this set here for your partner." Aki-chan said

as he placed the final card key and manual key on a tray at the end of the counter.

"Client." I said.

"Nani?" Aki-chan squeaked. He may have been younger than I thought.

"Matsumoto-sama is my client. Not partner." I said.

"Oh, you seemed much closer on the train. My mistake, I apologize." Aki-chan was polite.

"Don't worry about it. So how do we get to this room?" I asked.

"Forget about that, I want to show Miss Matsumoto my park." The elder Sano's voice filled the space as he announced his intentions.

"I'll go set up your rooms, if you like? I had the porter send your bags on from the train. Everything will be ready once Ojisan brings you back." Aki-chan said.

"You seem sure of that, Sano-san. Do you often escort guests from the train to the MiraCoast?" I asked. Something didn't feel right to me, and not just because my holiday was first hijacked by Reiko and Miki and now by a boy barely out of his teens and his half-blind grandfather.

"No, not at all. Before I got the job selling eki-ben, I was the porter for the MiraCoast. I escorted guests and their baggage from the train the couple times a year when we were open. The rest of the time I helped Ojisan with keeping the park running and in good condition." Aki-chan replied.

"Naruhodo. Miki, let's get this over with, ok?" I turned to my operations manager and was disappointed to see an enthusiastic gleam in her eyes.

"Oh, yes. Right away, Zach-kaicho." Miki said as she took off after Reiko and the elder Sano.

"Naruhodo." I said to no one in particular as I followed my client and my employee into the old amusement park.

The old sea park was spectacular, even in its current state of benign decay. The central lake dominated the view with an enormous volcano rising from the far side of man-made water feature. Shows used to take place on the water. I remembered them from when I was a child. Men, women, and yuru-charas would cavort on boats and jet skis, fireworks would be send aloft, and lights would turn the lake into a stage.

The volcano was still impressive. It was actually a thrill ride. The Jules Verne themed roller coaster took you to the center of the earth and spat you out with a gout of flame from the top of the ersatz volcano. I loved it as a child, with a love I never felt for anything ever again. If I was honest, I wanted to avoid being here and seeing the volcano again. I feared for the state of the park after the 3rd Great Kanto Earthquake. The news had broadcast images of the breach in the sea wall after the disaster. Back then, it was like the only safe part of my childhood had died, and I didn't want to have a reunion with childhood's corpse.

The sight ahead of me proved I had been wrong. Except for the gently listing replica Spanish galleon docked at the base of Jules Verne's volcano, everything was just as I remembered.

"We should go to the far side of the lake. I've been working on the roller coaster all year in anticipation of obon." The elder Sano said. He seemed proud. I, however, was confused.

"Ojisan, why for obon? I would have thought you would work on floating lanterns or something like that for the ancestors." I asked, my curiosity was not as in awe of the sight as was my heart.

"Oh? Because when the quake struck ten years ago, Jules Verne's volcano was the only ride where everyone survived. No casualties. I plan on using the Tarrasque as a giant lantern to celebrate those who lived and honor those who died." The old man said.

"Naruhodo. No one died on the thrill ride? What about the gondolas? Surely it wasn't the only ride with no casualties?" I asked.

"My poor, deluded boy. The gondolas were the worst. The waves swept three full boats out to sea when the barrier wall broke. No one was recovered." The old man fell visibly sadder. I had touched something deep inside him. Something deep and filled with sorrow.

"Nice, kaicho." Miki hit me hard on the shoulder. I deserved that one, even if I didn't know what I was saying to the old man was hurtful.

"I'm sorry, Sano-san. I didn't mean to bring up old memories." I apologized.

"Zach, why don't you head back. I'm the one who wants to see the animatronics, not you." Reiko said as she took the old man's hand in her own.

"Naruhodo."

Fire erupted from the top of Jules Verne's volcano. A giant lantern indeed. The old man would be proud. It was spectacular, and I swore I felt the heat from across the lake. Rather than being happy, the elder Sano turned around quickly to look at the volcano.

"That wasn't supposed to happen. Not yet. I have to get up there." He said with a certain panic in his voice. We didn't say a word, we just followed him as he ran to a small door on the side of one of the fake Italian buildings.

"Come with me, this is the service tunnel entrance." Sano said.

We followed him into the building and down a couple flights of metal stairs. There was a miniature train car at the bottom, waiting for us to climb in and set off. We did.

"Servicing the park starts with the trains in the service tunnels. Makes it easier to get everywhere." Sano said.

"I bet it helps with all the actors and yuru-chara that worked here." Miki said. Her eyes twinkled in the dim lights. Miki was on an adventure. My feelings of unease grew stronger.

"You've done a magnificent job, Ojisan." Reiko said as the electric car whisked us down the tunnel at a brisk rate of speed. In a scant few minutes we came to a stop next to another set of metal stairs going up. The tunnels continued on, but we stepped out of the car. A sensor somewhere turned the lighting up and I could read the sign next to the stairs. It read 'Center of the Earth' in Japanese, Chinese, and English.

"I only routed power to this section of the maintenance tunnels. I wasn't planning on running the other attractions." Sano said.

Sano started up the stairs, moving like a man half his age. I was struggling to follow him, so strong was his determination. We eventually came to a landing, then ran down a corridor to a control room. Sano got out a key and unlocked the door. A blue and white stuffed duck hung from the key. Sano certainly kept the themes of the park alive.

Miki gasped out loud as we entered the control room. Computers, servers, and routers were humming with power and activity. None of them should have been working, and yet the electronics appeared to be in perfect condition.

"This is amazing. It all works. How does it all work?"

Miki said as loud as she could to get over the hum of the electronics.

"The mountain. There is enough material above us to shield the computer controls. We're in a giant Faraday cage." Sano said.

Reiko went up to one monitor. There were LCD screens all along one wall to monitor the entire ride. Most of the images were static, but one showed motion.

"Ojisan, which part of the ride is this?" Reiko asked, jabbing her finger at the LCD monitor.

"That should be the Tarrasque. It's the climax of the ride. That's also where the fire erupts from the top of the volcano. Why? What do you see?" The elder Sano was squinting at the image, but his eyes were just not up to the job.

"The Tarrasque is moving. I thought the fire was one shot when the ride ran past the animatronic creature?" Reiko asked.

"It is." I said. As a child, the Tarrasque was my favorite part of my favorite ride. The car malfunctions and you are sent hurting through the earth. You come out at the Tarrasque. It's a giant half-dragon, half-centipede monster sitting on a pile of leathery eggs that seethe as the Tarrasque breathes fire at the car and the riders narrowly escape certain death. Or so it seemed to my ten-year-old self.

"Then what is on fire in front of the machine?" Reiko jabbed her finger at the LCD, tapping the screen with one sharp fingernail.

"I don't know. Nothing should be on fire." Sano said.

"Zach-kaicho. Is that what I think it is?" Miki said next to me.

"Naruhodo. It looks like a person." I said.

"People shouldn't be on fire." Reiko said.

A burst of flame came from the Tarrasque and the body moved. Whoever it was might have still been alive. I went to the door.

"Sano-san, how do we get to the Tarrasque? Whoever that is might be alive. We have to get them out of there." I shouted.

"Turn right, go to the end of the hall and climb the ladder. I'll try to shut it off." Sano said as he started typing at a keyboard just below the monitor for the Tarrasque.

"I'll try to help Ojisan." Reiko said, pulling up a chair beside the old man.

"Miki, let's go. Grab a fire extinguisher if you see one." I started out the door and down the hall to the right. We had to run fast.

I knew we were getting close when the smell hit my nose. I knew it was too late before we got to the top of the ladder. The smell of charred meat was far too strong. The service lights were already on in the ride. The Tarrasque was still moving, but no flames came from its mouth. In front of the Tarrasque, a body was trussed up like nothing I had ever seen before. It was suspended over the tracks and still burning. Nothing moved but the flames.

Miki came up behind me and began discharging a fire extinguisher on the corpse. She had stopped to take it off the wall before we started up the ladder. I looked around and saw another extinguisher, took it off the wall and helped put out the remaining flames.

It was definitely a person. Definitely dead. The fire had badly burned the body, but the legs seemed untouched. It was a woman. A woman wearing ancient Juan Baptiste shoes. I knew those shoes.

"Miki. Get to a phone. Call the police. After that, call

my lawyer. Asuka will want to know about this." I instructed my employee.

"Zach-kaicho, what's going on. You look like you've seen a ghost. Do you recognize the body?" Miki asked.

"Yeah. It's a lawyer. Never caught her name. I called her Razor Suit." I said.

"That's a strange name, Zach. You ok?" Miki asked.

"Before it burned, her suit had the sharpest, best creases I'd ever seen. So fine, you could cut your eyes on them."

THE ALIBI, THE LAWYER, AND THE ARREST

"Chief Detective Inspector Hara would like to speak with you now, Mr. Lejeune." The uniformed officer, Sato-san, said from the doorway of our hotel room.

Hara and her officers had arrived less than ten minutes after Miki called for help. Days were slow in Maihama, I guessed. I also guessed that at least two full kobans showed up to document the crime scene. The defunct sea park was lousy with uniforms and no one was paying for a room. The elder Sano would have been disappointed if there wasn't a dead body haunting his thoughts. He paced most of the time, talking about the ride and its spotless history; now ruined.

"Mr. Lejeune, why are you here?" CDI Hara asked.

I sat in the unoffered chair. We were meeting in the lobby since it was the central ingress to the park. Hara probably wanted to dangle freedom in front of the witnesses in case one of us was the culprit.

"The train to Chiba broke down. The steward offered for us to stay here. Where's my lawyer?" I said.

"Why do you want your lawyer, Mr. Lejeune?" Hara

continued her line of questioning. She was fishing. There were no clues to be had yet. The mobile forensic team would be about their business for some time. Burned bodies obscure evidence well.

"I think it's a good idea to have my lawyer on hand when there are dead bodies in my vicinity." I knew I was saying too much, but I wanted to help. I'm not fond of the better side of my personality, but you can't change who you are without changing more than you bargained for; so I said too much to the detective.

"Are you often in the vicinity of dead bodies, Mr. Lejeune?" CDI Hara continued. My other talent, self-preservation, kicked in. It was time to stop talking.

"More than I care to be. Tell me, do you often come to the park, or is this a special trip just for us?" I didn't follow self-preservation's hint. Hara pulled a chair up in front of me and turned it around. She sat in the backwards chair and leaned into me, face to face.

"Do I need to make a special trip for you, Mr. Lejeune? Or would you like to confess anything to me right now?" Crap. Self-preservation was not happy with me. Apparently I don't actually have a talent for that self-preservation.

"I think I would like to wait until my lawyer arrives, if that's alright with you, CDI Hara?" I said. A little late, but at least I finally said it.

"CDI Hara." Officer Sato walked up to the detective as she stared into my eyes. I felt like a small, helpless animal, and CDI Hara was a cat.

"Yes?" Hara prompted her man.

"The forensic team has the time of death." Sato held out a slip of paper to Hara, and she looked at it just by moving her eyes. He held the paper in place until Hara shifted her eyes back to me.

"You were boarding the train at Tokyo Eki around 10:15 this morning, isn't that right?" Hara asked me. I looked around for my lawyer. I just moved my eyes, I didn't want to move too suddenly with a cat ready to pounce. I nodded.

"Good. Seems you're probably just a necrophiliac. The victim was killed between 9 and 10. No way you could get from here to central Tokyo in time to board your train." Hara smiled gently. She must have found something funny about the situation that honestly didn't register to me.

"And that makes me a necrophiliac?" I asked.

"I checked on you before Office Sato called you to this interview, Mr. Lejeune. We have tied you to no less than 6 deceased persons in the last few months. Either you are extremely unlucky, a serial killer, or a necrophiliac." Hara smiled more broadly.

"And since I didn't kill any of them, you skipped bad luck and went straight to sex with dead bodies because that's exactly what one does when ritualistically murdering a woman using jets of fire and robot monsters on a roller coaster? How did I miss that logic?" I gave up pretending I had any inclination towards self-preservation.

"Hardly. I just don't believe in bad luck." Hara laughed. Great. Where was CDI Jones when I needed his workman-like abuse?

"Now that you have established my client's alibi, can we move on from this unfortunate situation?" My lawyer's voice rang out from the front entrance of the MiraCoast hotel.

"CDI Hara, meet my bengoshi, Konno Asuka." I smiled at the detective.

"Oh, we've met. She's the one that brought me the timeline on you and the information on your recent run-ins with dead bodies." Hara said.

"Wait, what? Konno-san, care to explain what's going on?" I looked at my lawyer in disbelief.

"I needed to establish your alibi, Lejeune-sama. In this situation, being up front and open is the best policy." Konno said as she walked up to me. Konno ruffled my hair as I sat in the chair.

"How long have you been here?" I asked, realizing then she didn't just arrive.

"About an hour. I headed out to get you when I heard about the train accident. I didn't want you in Reiko and Miki's clutches without your mother to keep them in line." Asuka said.

"What are you talking about?" I asked. Hara laughed.

"He's just like you said." Hara got up and walked over to the hotel counter with Officer Sato.

"What's Hara talking about?" I asked.

"Nothing you need to worry your pretty little head about, Zach-chan. Now, what the hell is going on in this decrepit amusement park?" Asuka sat in Hara's vacated chair.

"You remember the government lawyer you used to work for? Well, she's dead. Someone strung her up and burned her to a crisp in the Jules Verne ride." I explained to my lawyer.

"What? Do you mean Ishida-san or Morita-san? Those are the only two female government bengoshi I've worked with recently." Asuka was genuinely surprised.

"I don't know her name. She wore vintage Juan Baptiste and dressed like a predator. She was sharp, creased, and looked a little deadly. I just called her the 'Razor Suit.'" I rattled off what I knew about the lawyer.

"Ishida-san. She loved those shoes. Had surgery to make sure they fit perfect. On the shoes, not her feet. She was perfect in her own mind." Asuka said.

"Ishida-san. Sure. I only ever met her that one time when I first met you. I thought you were the junior partner." I said.

"What have you gotten into, Zach? Don't you think it's a little coincidental? How come you keep getting wrapped up with all these bizarre dead bodies?" Asuka whispered at me fiercely.

"Don't ask me, I've never had a dead body problem before." Strictly speaking, that was a lie.

"Yeah, right? I think I know why some people call you a nogitsune. I should start charging you by the body instead of by the hour, Zach." Asuka said.

An officer walked into the lobby and stepped in close to CDI Hara. They spoke briefly before Hara, Sato, and the new officer turned and headed out of the lobby and deeper into the hotel.

"What was that about?" I asked.

"Probably nothing good. Tell me now, you have nothing to do with this, do you Zach-chan?" Asuka asked in a serious voice.

"Of course not, counselor. You should know by now, I don't have a penchant for murder. Murder has a penchant for me." I said. It sounded better in my head. Asuka seemed to think so too. She crinkled her nose and frowned.

"Crap, Zach-chan. You are a handful, you know that?" Asuka got up and walked over to the counter. She rang the bell by slapping it five times in a row. No one came to answer her call.

"As far as I can tell, it's a skeleton crew here." I said loudly.

Asuka leaned over the counter, saw something and reached for it. She came back with an old telephone, picked up the receiver and dialed a number. A few minutes and a heated conversation later, Asuka came back and sat with me.

"Mr. Lejeune, I cannot represent you in this matter. I have called a colleague whom I trust. He has offered to represent you at no uncertain cost to myself. Please, do what he tells you? None of your usual coy games, ok?" Asuka said. All business and very rehearsed. I was sure they taught speeches like the one my counselor had just delivered at law school.

"What? Why? You're my lawyer, Konno-sama. I don't want anyone else." I protested.

"Can't happen, Zach-chan. I knew Ishida. I know you. There's a history there. I can't get involved in this. Not anymore. It isn't safe for either of us." Asuka said. I had never seen my lawyer worried before. Asuka was worried now, and not just because she knew Ishida-san. Something was different. Something I would have to get to the bottom of at some point, but probably not right now.

"Who is the bengoshi?" I asked.

"Okamoto Aoki. The senior Okamoto, not the playboy." Asuka said as if dropping the name of the most expensive political lawyer in Forgotten Tokyo was a casual referral.

I said nothing.

"Zach-chan, are you still in there?" Asuka asked, tilting her head to the side like a bird.

I said nothing.

"Lejeune Zakurai, answer your lawyer? Client? Hello?"

I said nothing.

"Fine. You have the best lawyer in the country. See if I care." Asuka stood up and walked away.

"Asuka. I have the best lawyer in the country. Okamoto is an ass. You are twice the lawyer he is." I said.

"Crap. You have a history with him. That's why he drove such a hard bargain. What did you do to Okamoto the Shark?" Asuka practically yelled at me.

"Nothing. Why did I have to do something to that jerk?" I yelled back.

"Oh, I don't know, perhaps because he asked for my dignity instead of just money? Zach, you really are a bastard, aren't you?" Asuka stood in front of me, fire burning in her eyes.

"Your dignity? I never asked for another lawyer, Asuka-sama. You're my lawyer, not Okamoto. Not after what he did to me." I was angry. I would never have asked for Okamoto Aoki, the senior or the junior. We had a history. Apparently so did Konno.

"I can't. Like it or not, I have a conflict of interest when it comes to Ishida. You need representation, and not some half-assed rental lawyer." Asuka shouted in my face.

"You're a rental lawyer!" I shouted back.

"No Zach, I'm not! I'm a goddamn prodigy." Asuka blushed and turned away from me.

"What?" I said, just above a whisper.

"You heard me. Rising young star. Okamoto's mystery woman from the countryside. That's your lawyer, Lejeune Zakurai. The Shark's Egg." I could swear I heard a sob from my lawyer. Impossible.

"You were the apprentice? The negotiator Okamoto brought in to get the Treaty of Acapulco signed by all seven nations?" I asked.

Asuka nodded and said nothing.

I tried to process the new information. Asuka was the prodigy. The Shark's Egg. When the seven industrialized nations couldn't agree to manage themselves after the Drift, The Shark's Egg brought them all to the table and got the Treaty of Acapulco signed and made into law. She disappeared soon afterwards, and some people figured it was all a ruse by Okamoto. He had a flair for the dramatic. Now my lawyer said she was The Shark's Egg.

"Why are you working for a loser like me?" I asked. Asuka slapped me. I hadn't expected to get slapped by my rental lawyer for asking a question. Would the surprises never end?

"Lover's spat, Mr. Lejeune?" CDI Hara said as Asuka stomped out of the lobby.

"Hardly. My lawyer just dumped me." I grumbled.

"I stand by my first opinion. Lover's spat." Hara said.

"As a client." I said, "Are you a secret pervert or just a little eechi and desperate?"

"Ah, Jones warned me you had a tongue on you, Lejeune." Hara continued, "Now why don't you come with me and we can have a nice little chat?"

"How do you know CDI 'Jones' Watanabe?" I asked, "And we already spoke, Hara. I just want to go back to my office and forget any of this ever happened."

"That's not possible. Could you come with me, now?"

"No, CDI Hara. I can *not* come with you now. I just lost my lawyer and my new lawyer hasn't arrived yet. And I want to know how you know CDI Watanabe." I was angry at the situation and Hara was a convenient target for my wrath.

"CDI Jones called when he heard my case involved you. He was afraid you would take advantage of me with your words. He was wrong, as usual." Hara explained.

"That doesn't answer my question." I said.

"I know." Hara replied.

"Fine. What do you want this time, Hara?" I gave up. I wasn't involved in this murder, so why not help the detective out?

"We found something. I need you to explain it." Hara said as she led me over to the hotel counter.

"What could I possibly explain?" I asked, shaking my head in disbelief.

"We found a device in your bag. A transmitter. I want to know how it got there and what you did with it." Hara said as she placed a box on the counter. It was the size of a child's kokeshi doll. Three toggle switches were built into its front plate and an antenna poked out the back of the device.

"I've never seen it before in my life." I said honestly.

"It was in your bag. Wrapped in your fundoshi. Sato didn't appreciate your wrapping methods." Hara smiled like a cat again. She held her hand out to Sato. He placed a bundle of cloth in her hand and Hara let it trail out onto the counter next to the device.

"Are you trying to annoy me by messing with my underwear? Seriously, this is cheap and petty, even for police in the countryside." I prefer my clothes neat, clean, and pressed. I spend a large portion of Sunday mornings ironing, pressing, and generally arranging my clothes into an agreeable presentation. Hara just wrinkled and dirtied one of my favorite fundoshi by dumping it on the counter like a dead animal.

"Empty your pockets, Mr. Lejeune, if you please?" Hara said. It wasn't a question.

"Fine." I took out my wallet, my handkerchief, and some spare change and placed it all on the counter.

"That too." Hara said, glancing down at my vest pocket.

I said nothing and just frowned. I took my pocket watch out of my vest pocket and placed it on the handkerchief.

Something else rolled out from beneath the pocket watch. Hara let it wobble on the counter before it fell over and stopped. It was a round disk with a single red button placed right in the center. The button seemed to be the diaphragm type made of spring steel that clicks when you push it.

"Well, well." Hara said.

"I've never seen that before in my life." I objected.

"Indeed." Hara said.

"I'm serious. It isn't mine."

"It was in your pocket, Lejeune."

"It's not mine. I don't even know what it is." I protested.

"Shall we find out, then?" Hara said, smiling, "Sato, are we clear?"

"Yes, ma'am." Officer Sato replied.

Hara picked up the disk and held it at her eye level. She looked me dead in the eyes and pressed the button. The toggle switches actuated on the transmitter device. I could hear the flames erupt from the ersatz volcano across the lake. My shoulders sank as I realized I was being framed.

"Mr. Lejeune Zakurai, I am placing you under arrest for the kidnapping, torture, and murder of Ishida Chiaki. You have the right to tell me how, why, and what you did to her. I appreciate full confessions and will make sure you spend the rest of your days walking back and forth in a 2-tatami room in a prison in Hokkaido." Hara said as Sato pulled my arms back and placed shackles around my wrists.

"I didn't do any of that. I'm being framed. I've never seen any of this garbage before, and I don't wrap things in perfectly pressed clothing. That is a travesty." I said. No one seemed to care.

"You know what's a travesty?" Sato whispered in my ear, "That a sick monster like you doesn't get executed for that horror show you put on up there. I've never seen anything like that outside of an American movie."

"Thanks for the impartiality, Sato. I didn't do this. I want to talk to my lawyer when he gets here. Okamoto the senior, not the playboy!" I said as Sato took me away to the waiting police car.

"What's going on?" I heard Miki call as they took me out of the hotel.

"I'm being framed. Get to Konno-san. She can help. Make sure Reiko stays out of trouble." I yelled back.

"Rokkai!" I heard Miki yell as they pushed me into the back of the police car. I ducked low. I've been put in police cars before. If you don't watch yourself, your head always seems to find the pointy part of the metal, almost like it was intentionally placed there just for your head.

ASUKA, REIKO, AND MIKI

"Lejeune, you have a visitor." Officer Sato said from outside my cell.

"About time. Send Okamoto-sama in." I was ready to confront my unwanted lawyer. When Sano Aki walked in, it surprised me.

"And what brings you here, steward?" I asked from the chair inside my cell. The younger Sano said nothing as he pulled a chair up to the cell bars and sat down. I wanted to hear what he had to say. I knew he played a role in framing me, but I needed to hear from him to determine how big of a role he had played.

"Lejeune Zakurai. You upset my grandfather with what you did to his favorite attraction." Sano said.

"Are we going to play dumb, Aki-chan?" I looked at the barely post-adolescent man with a blank look.

"Not at all. I just want to set the scene." Aki revealed a small disk he carried in his hand. He pressed it like a button. Nothing seemed to happen.

"What was that? Not a remote like the one you planted

on me when we were on the train?" I led with what I knew. Better to get the boy talking. The young could be careless.

"Not exactly. This disk just blanks the video camera. Now we can talk. I have a message for you, Lejeune-san." Aki said, not even trying to deny his role in my frame up.

"A message? Who are you speaking for, not your grandfather?" I wanted him to talk more. Youthful indiscretions could be worth encouraging.

"The message is 'Falstaff sends his regards.' I hope that gives you some comfort." Aki said. I had no idea what he was talking about, and I said as much.

"You could have just sent a letter. You didn't have to kill Ishida-san. What did she ever do to you and this Falstaff person?" I tried to draw him out.

"Killing the lawyer was part of the deal. One dead lawyer, one delivered message, and one hundred million yen." Aki stood up.

"What? One hundred million yen? You killed that woman for money?" I couldn't believe my ears, "Why would you do that? Do you think this is a movie?"

"Not at all. One hundred million yen will save the park. It will save my ojisan. I'd gladly kill a few more lawyers to save him. Luckily, Falstaff just wanted you to take the fall for it. Consider yourself lucky, Mr. Lejeune." Aki said as he walked out.

"What was that all about?" I muttered to myself. I figured out that Aki had to be the one who planted the disk on me when the train accident occurred. I had a hunch he was also responsible for the accident itself. He probably used his radio to call ahead after he sold us the eki-ben. An accomplice must have dropped the hay bales onto the tracks. He either faked the injury or fell when the train stopped. Either way, he took advantage of the situation and planted the transmitter on me when he stuffed my watch into my vest pocket.

Aki was also responsible for planting the other device. He had our bag brought to the hotel and took care of placing them in our rooms personally when we were on the tour of the park. I just needed to prove it. I needed to investigate, but I was stuck in a cell, under arrest for a crime I didn't commit. I needed my lawyer, Konno Asuka.

"Zach-kaicho, are you ok?" Miki ran to my cell. A second surprise.

"Miki, why are you here?" I asked.

"Why would you even ask that, boss? Asuka-kun told us they arrested you. Reiko is here too. The police are making her take off her heels. They don't want her to do anything violent." Miki said.

"Reiko? Violent? I expect that from you, but from her?" I was fairly certain Miki wasn't joking.

"Ha. For someone you know so well, you sure as hell don't really understand that woman, do you Zach-kaicho?"

"Zach-chan!" Reiko ran in behind Miki and thrust her hand through the bars. Her finger pointed at my nose, scant millimeters away from scratching me.

"Matsumoto-sama, is there a problem?" I said as I avoided her jabbing finger.

"You're in jail. Of course something is wrong. What did you do? Did you kill that woman? Why didn't you let me settle your score for you?" Reiko said accusingly.

"You should know me better than that, Matsumoto-sama. I don't settle scores and I don't turn perfectly good lawyers into ebi-fry." I said.

"You should know our Zach is not nearly nefarious enough for something like what happened to Ishida-san." Konno Asuka said from behind Reiko.

"Well, we're all here. How do we get you out, Zach-kaicho?" Miki sat in Sano's vacated chair.

"We don't. The case is solid." Konno said.

"It's a frame-up, counselor." I replied.

"Obviously, client. The question is, who did it and how do we prove it?" My lawyer was sharp. She knew it was a frame.

"It was Sano. He framed me. Someone hired him to do it for a lot of money. I even know how and when he did it. What I don't know is why." I said.

"Well, the boss-man has solved the case. Just tell the men in uniform and let's get you out of here." Miki smiled.

"It's not that simple. They found the disk on Zach-chan and the transmitter in his bag. We only have his word that Sano Aki framed Zach. We need evidence." Asuka explained to Miki.

"It took some skill to rig up that Tarrasque to torch poor Miss Ishida," Reiko said, "I could have done it. So could the grandfather. Could Aki-chan pull it off?"

"I don't know. We need to prove that. We also need to find out why he needed the money." I said.

"Well, I was looking over the computers. Most of them are vintage, but some components are modern. Expensive. Maybe it was debt?" Miki leaned forward. It piqued her interest.

"Maybe. If it is just about the money, then we need to know who's behind Aki. He gave me a message. Said 'Fal-staff sends his regards.' I don't know anyone named Falstaff." I let my words hang in the air to be absorbed. We needed ideas, and these were the three smartest people I knew.

"I could talk to the grandfather. He seems to like me

well enough, and he's definitely shaken by the murder. I don't think he had anything to do with it." Reiko offered.

"I'll see if I can poke around the control room. The computers had to be compromised to control the Tarrasque. Maybe the kid was sloppy?" Miki was on-board. I looked at my lawyer.

"What?" Konno Asuka asked.

"Can't you do something too, counselor?" I asked.

"I told you. I have a conflict of interest. I got you a new lawyer, Zach-chan. Honestly, I shouldn't even be in here with you three. I should probably go talk to CDI Hara. Explain some things about Ishida-san and me. Bye, Zach-sama." Asuka turned and walked out.

"Some help she is." Miki snorted.

"She called you -sama. Zach-chan, you don't think?" Reiko looked at Miki, then at me.

"Yes, yes, I think so. Konno-san only calls clients -sama. Asuka is on the case. Now get going. Come back when we learn something. I'll probably be right here." I said. Reiko and Miki headed out. They had to do my job for me while I was in a cell. No talent was going to help me. Everything that could go wrong already went wrong. I certainly didn't need any help on the bad luck front.

I kept sitting and thinking. Who was Falstaff? Why did he want me framed? I didn't have any answers. I must have sat for a few hours. I could tell when I tried to stand and failed. Blood wasn't circulating in my legs very well.

"Don't get up on my account, Mr. Lejeune." A man's voice said from outside my cell. I looked up to see Okamoto. The elder Okamoto. Lovely.

"Hello, Shark. I would say I'm happy to see you, but neither of us enjoys hearing lies." I frowned. How long had he been sitting there while I was thinking? I didn't know.

"Nogitsune. I see your tongue hasn't been dulled as much as your wits." Okamoto was old but still sharp. He was old when I first met him before the Drift.

"What did you extort from my rental bengoshi, Shark?" I asked. No sense in sparring verbally with the old man. I was bound to be the loser in that fight.

"None of your business, Nogitsune. Sufficed to say, she had something I wanted. You were the price. She must think highly of you. Does she know the truth?" Okamoto didn't waste time on pleasantries.

"No. If you tell her, I may have to break our bargain." I said. It was a threat, and Okamoto knew it.

"Never crossed my mind, Nogitsune. A bargain is a bargain. My silence for your silence. I just wanted to know if she was as important to you as you are to be to my little Egg." Okamoto reached a papery hand into his suit pocket. He wore a three piece suit of exceptionally high quality and fit. No doubt it cost a fortune. When he withdrew his hand, it held a pen and a small notebook. I didn't need to see it to know it was coming. Okamoto always took precise notes.

"Now, tell me what happened. Leave nothing out, Nogitsune, or I shall walk out on this case and let you rot in perpetuity."

I told Okamoto everything. He didn't ask questions and left when I completed my story. I heard him grunt from the hallway just as Miki raced in to see me.

"I found it. The kid was sloppy. He just wrote a script in some old language called Python. Almost like reading plain text. English plain text, but so what? Who was that geezer?" Miki was out of breath. My employee was barrel chested from training as a boxer. I bet she could have been a prizefighter. Miki must have run all the way from the park to be out of breath.

"That's my new lawyer. Okamoto the Shark." I said.

"I like your real lawyer. The Shark looks like he would fold if I pinched him too hard." Miki smiled and genuine smile of joy. She had found something good.

"You seem happy. What did you find, Miki?" I asked.

"The script. It was written in a development environment." she replied.

"And that means something to you?" It meant nothing to me.

"Silly boss-man. Sano wrote it in his own development environment. It has his name registered in the program. He signed his own malicious script and probably didn't even know it." Miki smiled "And that's not all. He commented the hell out of it. Documented everything he wrote. What it did, why he was doing it. The whole script is explained in black and white."

"Would someone like me understand it? You know, a non-nerd?" I asked.

"Absolutely. You're cleared, boss!"

"Not quite." Asuka was back. Cold water on Miki's celebration.

"What do you mean? We have him in his own words." Miki protested.

"Your find proves the script was written in Sano Aki's program, not that Sano Aki wrote the program. Anyone with access could have written it." Asuka was right. The evidence was circumstantial, not conclusive. We needed more.

"I see you met with Okamoto-san. What did he say?" Asuka looked at me with cold eyes.

"The Shark said the price you paid was too high." I looked back into my lawyer's eyes, "Care to tell me what he wanted from you, counselor?"

"No. It's personal. Stay out of it, Lejeune-sama. Please?" The last word was sincere. Konno Asuka didn't want me to know the value she put on me. I was willing to respect that.

"Oh, lover's spat." Miki said and was ignored.

"Zach-chan is my date this weekend. You girls had best remember that." Reiko broke the chill as she entered with a rolled up blueprint in her hands.

"What do you have there, Matsumoto-sama?" I asked.

"Jackpot. Plans for the modification of the Tarrasque and the truss system Sano used to murder Ishida-san." Reiko presented the plans triumphantly.

"Where did you find them?" I asked.

"In the rooms Aki-chan was responsible for right before he took the job as a train steward. It was only last week, did you know that? This was all a planned set-up from the start." Reiko unrolled the plans. At least a dozen large sheets were rolled up together. None of it meant anything to me. Reiko was the engineer, I was just the consultant.

"Anything incriminating?" Asuka asked.

"Only the entire working parameters for the transmitters, the animatronics, and the protocols to call some computer script. If only we had that, then we could show the entire process flow." Reiko explained.

"We have it." Miki said proudly.

"This is bad." Asuka said.

"What do you mean? How is finding this evidence bad?" I asked.

"That's just it, it isn't evidence anymore. Reiko took it from the scene. We would need the police to find it *in situ*. Now it's just something we claim is evidence. Sano can say we planted it to frame him. He could turn the tables on Zach. It could even make us into accomplices."

My lawyer explained. She was the best, and sometimes I hated that fact. We needed something more. We needed a video or a confession. A video and a confession would be best. An idea came to me. I looked closer at the plans. I recognized some details from when I was a net-drama star. Thrill rides are all about illusion, just like entertainment.

"Konno-san, can you get CDI Hara to take me to the MiraCoast? Can you get both Sano and his grandfather, too?" I asked.

"It would be a minor miracle, but perhaps I could. What do you have in mind?" she asked.

I pointed to the plans and explained my idea. At first Reiko thought I was crazy. Next Miki thought I was crazy and insisted machines did not work the way I was describing in my plan. I asked a few leading questions about the Python script. Computers really are not my forte, but I had a working knowledge of logic. I explained what I wanted each of them to do and how to do it.

"Now I see why Okamoto calls you a Nogitsune." Asuka said.

"Wild fox? Who calls my brilliant and crazy Zach-chan a wild fox?" Reiko seemed offended someone would give me a nickname she didn't approve of, but Miki just laughed.

"We can do this. Tell me you all think we can do this?" I asked the women.

"We can." All three said together.

"Can you pull off your part, Zach-kaicho?" Miki asked with worry in her voice.

"Miki-san, I was an actor long before I was Zach Tragic. Trust me, I've got this."

The women left to start their tasks. Brilliant, shrewd, and tough. I trusted them with my life, but if anything went wrong, it just might be my life that lost out. We would all find out in the morning. I fell asleep waiting for morning.

Morning came and went.

CDI Hara didn't show until 2:30 in the afternoon. She didn't say a word to me, but instructed Officer Sato to take me out of the cell and put me in a car. Sato did and then drove me back to the MiraCoast hotel. We must have taken the long way around because CDI Hara was waiting for us when we arrived. The detective had a flair for the dramatic.

"Why are we here, CDI Hara?" I asked.

"Crime, Lejeune. We are here because of crime." The detective said.

"I've been locked up all day and night. What possible crime could I have committed, CDI Hara?" I was revisiting an old role from before *Kudo's Repose*. I was in a comedy drama about a savant detective. Dumb on the outside but brilliant on the inside. The net-drama was panned as unrealistic. The critics thought my character should have been medicated.

"Come on. We're headed up to the control room. We found your accomplices there." Hara said. She walked me into the lobby where Sano Aki was waiting for us.

"You brought him? Is that wise, CDI Hara? Can't you just arrest the others and they can all rot in jail together?" Sano protested.

"Not until I get my confession. Come with us, I'm sure you'll want to hear them sing." Hara said as she marched us to the control room in Jules Verne's volcano.

"Mr. Lejeune, my men caught your accomplices, Konno, Matsumoto, and Miki here in the control room this morning. The last one doesn't seem to have a family name. I caught her playing with the computers." CDI Hara announced to the room. Konno Asuka, Matsumoto Reiko, and Miki were handcuffed and seated in cheap, metal chairs with police guarding them. The officer standing over Miki had a very large black eye.

Sano Aki stood off to the side. He was red with anger. I wasn't sure, but someone might have scratched his face, too. I looked at all the players in my drama. Only Sano Hideaki was missing. Perfect.

"Surely, I know nothing about this." I said. I made my words rounded and acted like a moonstruck child. It was a net-drama, after all.

"No? Then what were they doing in the control room with this?" CDI Hara waited for Officer Sato to step forward with the transmitter device in hand. Asuka had done it. Minor miracles did happen.

"What is that doing here?" Sano Aki drew in a breath when he saw the device. One of the toggle switches actuated without warning and Aki broke out in a sweat. I doubt anyone saw it except for me.

"What was that?" I asked, "Is the fire going to start again? I like fire. By the way, where's the old man?"

"He went up to the Tarrasque to inspect your accomplices' sabotage. I found that one messing with the gas effects. No doubt to clear your name, Mr. Lejeune." CDI Hara pointed at Reiko.

"Ojisan is with the Tarrasque?" Aki asked. CDI Hara ignored him. One monitor flickered to life as if on queue. It was.

"Is that the Tarrasque? Oh look, old man Sano is there." I said, narrating my play for the younger Sano's benefit. A second toggle actuated on the device.

Sano Aki made a strangled noise. He tried to grab the transmitter device from CDI Hara. She easily side-stepped his clumsy movements.

"You must stop it. The device is armed!" Sano Aki yelled. The third toggle actuated. Flames sprouted from the jets concealed in front of the Tarrasque. The monitor went blank. Aki-chan screamed.

"Ojisan. You killed my grandfather. You," Aki looked at me, "How did you do it? How did you hack my device?"

"Your device? What are you saying, Mr. Sano?" CDI Hara asked calmly. She was expecting something like this. Asuka convinced the detective to go along with our ruse. She wasn't the best lawyer in Japan for nothing. She convinced the CDI to go along with my scheme to uncover the killer with a promise of a confession and a video. Minor miracle indeed.

"Shut up!" Sano Aki struck out with a backhand across CDI Hara's face. The crack was too loud and slightly metallic. Hara hit the floor like a discarded kokeshi doll. I looked at Aki and the pistol he held in his hand. It wasn't a revolver like the police used, but a semiautomatic like the Yakuza and Americans packed. Unexpected.

"First one who moves, dies. I have enough bullets for all of you." Aki-chan announced.

"You little rat-dropping. If I wasn't handcuffed," Miki said with malice.

"You'd be the first one I shot." Aki-chan was waving the pistol like a Yakuza in a manga. Sideways and randomly.

"Why did you do it, Aki-san?" I asked. I slipped into my *Kudo's Repose* character. Everyone trusted my voice in that net-drama. Even crazy kids with loaded guns.

"I told you. I killed her for the money. One dead lawyer. One delivered message. One hundred million yen. You take the fall. It was all so easy. Now my grandfather is dead because of you." Aki was crying. He loved his ojisan.

"No. You made the device. You programmed the

computer. You did the killing. Not me." I said. Kudo calm, perfect for eliciting a confession.

"No! Yes, I did that. But not this. Why did you mess with the Tarrasque? Ojisan shouldn't have gone up there. He's going blind. I needed the money so he could retire, not burn up in flames."

"Did you get that?" I asked. Officer Sato increased the volume on his radio.

"Yes, Mr. Lejeune. We got it all on the camera. Sound was good too." said a voice over the air.

"Aki-chan, why?" The elder Sano's voice came over the radio.

"Ojisan? Your alive?" Aki asked through his tears. The boy's grip on the pistol was slack. My lawyer stood up and took a step towards the younger Sano.

"Stay back. I will shoot you." Aki made his threat. In a blink of an eye, Asuka's foot shot up and connected with Aki's hand, knocking the pistol into the air. Her other foot was in the air a moment later as she delivered a round-house kick to the boy's head, laying him out flat.

"I'm fine, Aki-chan, why?" The elder Sano said through the radio.

"I hate kids with guns." Asuka said as she walked away.

6

TRAGIC AT KANDA

THE POWER, THE REPORTER, AND THE SHOOTER

"What's going on here?" I asked Officer Kato as I looked up at the scaffolding surrounding the Akasaka koban.

"Ah, Lejeune-sama. Good to see you. We finally can afford to renovate the koban. Isn't it great?" Kato said proudly.

"Naruhodo. What are you changing?" I asked. The scaffolding was almost assembled; it completely obscured the koban from sight. Blue cloth panels, worn with use over time, were draped on the outside of the structure.

"Oh? I thought everyone knew? We're getting rid of the second floor interview rooms. The koban is going back to the way it used to be before the 3rd Great Kanto Earthquake." Kato said.

"Kitchens and beds upstairs? No more American-style rough-up rooms?" I didn't believe Kato.

"Yes. Finally. We get to be a normal police koban again. Once this is complete, only three Tokyo kobans will have interview rooms. Tokyo is getting back to normal." Kato said. The change meant a great deal to the young officer.

Kato was in his twenties. He would have been twelve or thirteen when the earthquake hit Tokyo. His entire life might as well have been lived in the ruins of the earthquake and the Drift seven years before that.

"Naruhodo." I was about to congratulate Officer Kato on the Akasaka koban's milestone koban when a siren pierced the morning calm. The power was about to go out.

"I need to prepare." Kato announced as if I didn't already know.

"Jya, ne." I said as I hastened to my office. Power outages were common in Forgotten Tokyo. Losing integrated circuit technology during the Drift had stalled advances in power generation and distribution. Once, the internet controlled everything. Now, with no mass telecommunication, no embedded microprocessors, and no internet, power generation and distribution was a purely electromechanical affair.

One consequence of using older technology was that power was limited to the complexity of the electromechanical systems of relays and switches. Once a week and sometimes more, everyone is an area would lose their power. Today was Minato's turn. Akasaka was a district in Minato, which was one of the twenty-three cities that made up Forgotten Tokyo.

I arrived at my office five minutes later. I had a stash of batteries charged and ready for power outages. My landlady frowned on it, but she always came to my office with bentos and other food when the power failed. As I rounded the top of the steps on the second floor, a woman who wasn't my landlady stood outside my office door. Waiting. Great, a reporter.

"If you're looking for Lejeune, tell me when you find that guy." I said to the reporter. I learned to recognize them after the incident at Skytree. There was just something in the way a reporter moved. The way they looked at you to determine what they needed to learn from you. I could see that in the woman's eyes. She needed something from Zach Lejeune. Something from me.

"Does he owe you something?" she asked. Lucky for me, the reporter didn't know my face.

"I can't begin to tell you." I said. Best to be non-committal as I looked up at the tall reporter. I noticed she had old scars on her arms. The scars spider-webbed across her skin like the sticky, stringy filaments of natto I liked for my breakfast. Swirling fermented soy beans into a sticky mass of ito on top of rice was immensely satisfying.

"What? The hero of Skytree is a deadbeat? That must be tough." I wasn't sure, but I thought she was playing with me. Something in her voice wasn't right. I looked at her closer. I try to remember the people who are after me. Usually they come for revenge or a refund. Reporters used to come for my story, then for the tragedy. The papers always enjoy a good tragedy.

At first I thought she was half my age, but as I looked closer, I suspected she might be older. Her hair was tied back and professional. The glint of an old-style socketed data port poked out from under her hair at the back of her neck. Those were all the rage years back. She dressed well, but the clothing was also not new. She clearly made a decent living, but not good enough to be frivolous. She coordinated the colors of her clothes as well; matched the dark blues with green highlights. Her purse was a large courier bag style mass. There were odd bulges that poked peaks into the black leather. Lighter, worn lines spidered across the skin of the bag. Neba neba, like the natto scars on her arms; yet it wasn't dry like an abused bag would be. She kept it well, but the bag must have been only one she used. The reporter made the most of what she had and took good care of old, well-used items. I would have to be careful.

"It is. What does he owe you?" I asked.

"Nothing. I just want to ask about Kanda. Do you know the story?" She asked. So she was here for the tragedy. The hero of Skytree's failure at Kanda. Only a few people remember the hero of Skytree is the same person who survived at Kanda seven years later. The papers ran the story for weeks. After Skytree ruined the internet, actual newspapers came back into vogue. We Japanese always had a love affair with paper, but by the time of the Drift, even we had nearly given up on dead tree news. Seven years later and it was as if newspapers had never gone out of fashion. Zach the hero of Skytree became Zach Tragic, sole survivor of Kanda during the 3rd Great Kanto Earthquake. I was front page news, twice. A regular celebrity. To be fair, I was a celebrity before the Drift and Skytree, but no one remembers me for being a twenty-something net-show idol. These days, no one really even remembers the net-shows.

"Never heard of it. Is that in Chiba?" I lied, "I hear they have good peanuts."

"The best. The fish is good too." The woman smiled. I didn't go in for romance and even now I'm not one for relationships, but I think I was beginning to like this nameless reporter. That was dangerous.

"Is it? Tell me more?" Keep her talking about anything but me.

"Oh, I think everyone knows about Chiba's reputation for fish. I'm more interested in what Mr. Lejeune thinks about the completion of the work at Kanda. What do you think about it?" She was good at deflecting my questions.

"The work at Kanda?" I played dumb, "What work are they doing at Kanda?"

"Restoration of the metro station is complete. Kanda Eki is opening again. Even the trains are running. And that's not all. The government will memorialize the victims of the earthquake. A spokesman said they recovered all the bodies except one." she said. She knew. I was being played.

"I have a curiosity. What's your name?" I asked.

"Ah, so we get to it now? I am Hamada Yu. Please to meet you, Lejeune Zakurai." Hamada said. And she called me by my net-show name. She knew who I was the whole time.

"You might as well come in, Hamada-san. Well done, leading me on." I said as I reached for the key in my pocket and unlocked my office door.

"Leading you on? Did I do that, Mr. Lejeune?" Hamada grinned and followed me in.

"Have a seat." I pointed to the chair in the corner. It was the bad chair. She didn't take it and instead looked around the room. Hamada took the good chair by the bookshelf and placed it to the side of my desk. I sat in the best chair, if you could call it that, behind my desk.

"Well, Mr. Lejeune, would you care to make a statement about Kanda?" she asked as she sat in the chair.

"No." I said.

"No? Is that all? What about the bodies?" Reporters always asked about the bodies.

"I said everything I had to say ten years ago." Please don't ask about him.

"Really? Well, how about just the one body?" She leaned forward slightly. I barely noticed it because she was very good at her job. But the anticipation of asking about him must have been more than her professionalism could bear.

"There were so many when Kanda fell, why would you care about anyone body? I'm sure the families care about them, but you? How does that make a story for you?" I tried being passive aggressive. Maybe she would get annoyed and leave.

"Oh, I don't think the family has cared about this body in a long time. The Myoujin, however, they still care. So do the bankers. They want him back." Hamada was definitely talking about him. I sighed. There was no way I was going to get out of this now. The question was, how much did I say before I tossed her out?

"Look, I don't know what you want me to say. Everything that happened at Kanda ten years ago is in the record. I stand by what I said. I did everything I could. I don't know why I was the only one to live." I lied. I knew exactly why I survived when the ceilings collapsed and crushed everyone else in the station. It was his fault.

"And yet everybody was recovered. Except his. Although I guess body is a bit generous. I just want to know what the hero of Skytree, what Zach Tragic, sole survivor of Kanda has to say about the fact that after all this time, after the full excavation and restoration of Kanda, the head of Taira no Masakado is nowhere to be found?" And there it was, right out of Hamada's mouth.

Taira no Masakado. Him. Hero, martyr, and traitor to the throne in Kyoto. Enshrined kami at Kanda Myoujin. Head interred at Otemachi. Missing since just before the 3rd Great Kanda Earthquake. The vengeful spirit that brings bad luck to those who are corrupt. And to those who offend him. Stolen by thieves and last seen by me, in the possession of the thieves as they tried to escape at Kanda Eki when the ceilings came crashing down.

"You should go. Now." I breathed slowly.

"I'm sorry, I didn't hear you." Hamada said. She probably didn't. I was mad and I get quiet when I'm mad.

"He said get your fancy butt out," Fukusawa said from the still open doorway, "Or I'll beat on it for fun."

"Pardon?"

"You heard me. Get out before I throw you out." Fukusawa was leaning against the doorjamb. She looked at the floor, then slowly raised her eyes to meet Hamada-san's gaze.

"You must be Fukusawa the Knife? Am I right?" Hamada stood and walked over to my landlady, "I'm Hamada Yu, pleased to meet you."

I would have sworn I heard Hamada smile as she offered her meishi.

I didn't hear what Fukusawa said in response. I honestly heard nothing because the pressure wave from the explosion overwhelmed everything as the windows shattered inward and rained glass over us all. I opened my eyes, but I could barely see Hamada lying on the floor by the door. I was on the floor. I blinked and the ringing in my ears responded by getting louder and more unbearable.

The sound and the pressure wave happened at the same time, so the explosion must have been very close. I tested myself by trying to kneel first, then stand. Everything seemed to be in the right places. I wasn't missing anything vital. The ringing didn't get better. I half-crawled over to Hamada, crouching as I went.

She was alive. I could see her breathing and as I approached, she curled into a ball. I spoke as loudly as I could before I reached out and touched Hamada's wrist. She flinched but didn't recoil. Her pulse was strong.

"Stay here." I yelled. Hamada flinched. At least she seemed to hear me.

I stepped over to the windows and looked out. Glass crunched under my feet. A giant gout of flame shot from the gas meter on the building across the street. I knew it must have been deliberate when I saw the flames. My talent can be very dangerous. I cause things around me to fail. Gas regulators and safety values included. I paid extra to live in this part of Akasaka in the form of triple redundant safety valves on all the gas supplies in the neighborhood. When you are a corollary to Murphy's law, you learn to accept the extra costs of living with precautions.

Someone had done this. Sabotaged my neighborhood. I ducked back down. If someone was making mischief, it probably involved me. I needed to call my lawyer. The phone was on my desk, or at least it had been before the explosion. Now, it was lying on the floor, off the hook. I crawled to the phone and closed the contacts to register the dial tone.

I couldn't hear the signal through the ringing in my ears, so I just dialed my lawyer. If she picked up, she would know it was me. Konno Asuka might be a rental bengoshi, but she was a damn good one. I yelled into the receiver.

"It's Zach. Someone blew up my neighborhood." I repeated myself three or four times. I wanted to make sure Konno-san got the message.

As I hung up the phone, I noticed the reporter trying to stand. I yelled at her to stay down. Hamada couldn't hear me. I felt something going wrong.

The heel on Hamada's shoe broke as she stood. She toppled as she lost her balance. I heard the crack and saw the sparks fly off the wall behind her as she regained her balance. Someone was shooting at my office. I moved as quickly as I could and tackled the reporter before she could stand up again.

Hamada was yelling at me and hitting me with her fists. She was not effective. I heard three more cracks. The gun shots were the only sound making it through the ringing.

I put my mouth right next to Hamada's ear and tried to speak loudly without yelling. I wanted her to hear what I said, but you really can't tell the volume of your voice when you can't hear it.

"Stay down. Someone is shooting at us."

"What?" I heard Hamada ask.

"Shooting. Guns. Someone is shooting guns at us."

"Why?"

"I don't know." I replied.

I looked around. I don't use weapons and guns are almost impossible to get in Forgotten Tokyo. My work is trouble-*shooting*, not trouble-*making*. I saw movement just outside my office.

Fukusawa was crouched outside the door. She pointed at me and then, when I met her gaze, tossed me a furoshiki wrapped bundle. She made a gesture around her face and mouth. I had no idea what she was doing. I picked up the bundle and untied the furoshiki. I understood.

I took one respirator and put it on over my face. It covered my mouth and nose as I pulled the canvas straps over my head. I covered the outlet vent and sucked in a breath. The cup of the respirator collapsed as I sucked in the air; I had a good seal. I placed the other respirator over Hamada's nose and mouth just as Fukusawa tossed two metal canisters into my office. Flame sprouted for the ends of the canisters, followed by a billowing, purple smoke.

Fukusawa was prepared for the next disaster, regardless of whether it was an earthquake, fire, or armed attack by unknown strangers. I had my money on earthquake and fire, but I still likely owed my landlady a couple thousand yen. We had a casual betting pool in the building. Fukusawa's money was on armed attack and kaiju.

Minutes passed. I stayed down, covering Hamada with my body in case the shooter made a personal appearance. More minutes passed. The sense of wrongness that accompanies my talent faded. I took a chance and looked up and around. Purple smoke was everywhere. No way the shooter could see through it. The smoke canisters were for signaling rescuers in case of a major disaster. Normal and infrared vision couldn't penetrate the smoke. It was made for maximum visibility.

The ringing gradually subsided, and I just felt as if my head was muffled in cotton. A commotion was audible on the steps outside my office. I tensed in case I needed to move. A light cut through the smoke, making everything light purple instead of dark purple. The smoke moved and swirled. Three shapes came into the office, one of them was waving a hand fan to displace the smoke. It was almost effective.

"Tragic, where are you?" Chief Detective Inspector Jones called out.

"Here," I yelled, holding up my arm, "We're over here."

CDI Watanabe 'Jones' Ichiro, Officer Kato, and my landlady with the hand fan, Fukusawa surrounded me and Hamada. Jones grabbed for my wrist, checking for a pulse. I'm sure it was beating faster than it should have.

"You ok? Who's this?" CDI Jones asked as he holstered his revolver.

"She's a reporter. Hamada Yu is her name. I think she's

ok." I said. The cotton feeling muffling my head seemed to fade.

"Kato, check the rest of the room." CDI Jones ordered.

"Did you get the guy?" I asked.

"What guy? The shooter? Who ever was shooting up my patch got away clean. Probably when Fukusawa tossed in the smoke cans. She probably saved your life, Tragic." Jones said without rudeness or sarcasm. My detective was learning, I guess.

"The office is clear, sir." Kato said.

"We need to get them checked out, Jones." Fukusawa-san said.

"Can you move, Tragic? What about the reporter?" Jones asked me.

"Yeah, I think we can move. The only thing broken is Hamada's shoe. You sure the shooter's gone? I don't feel like exploring alternate methods of breathing."

THE STATION, THE TUNNEL, AND THE LOCKED DOOR

A few cuts and scrapes were all Hamada and I suffered. My office windows were a total loss. The bullets didn't do much to the concrete walls. We were lucky. The bullet fragments Officer Kato recovered were from a long rifle. We wouldn't have survived getting shot with a rifle at close range.

CDI Jones watched over us at Toranomon Byoin. The hospital was a shadow of its former self, but it was still a very competent institution. It was also across the street from the scaffold enclosed Akasaka koban.

"Tragic, any idea what is going on? The gas explosion alone could have destroyed the entire street." CDI Jones asked me.

"I couldn't say. I was just telling that reporter to leave when everything went sideways." I replied.

"I can hear you, you know. I have a name." Hamada said from the other side of the drawn curtain.

The doctor was bandaging Hamada's wounds. They already took care of my wounds, and CDI Jones and I were simply waiting for Hamada to be treated and released.

Jones wanted our statements, but with the koban under renovation, he talked to us at the hospital. I liked to think he was also looking out in case the attempted killer returned.

"What did she want, anyway?" Jones asked, ignoring Hamada's voice.

"They finished the work on Kanda Eki. She wanted to get a reaction out of me." I said.

"Why? The government's been working on the station at Kanda for ten years. Why would anyone care what you think about a public works project?" CDI Jones was new to the Akasaka koban. He must not have bothered to read my entire file. He knew I was at Kanda when the 3rd Great Kanto Earthquake destroyed the station. He knew I was the only survivor. When my first lawyer tried to frame me for murder, Jones used that incident to railroad me into a confession. I suggested he read the entire report, but he hadn't done so.

"Watanabe-san, learn to read the entire report. You know I survived at Kanda. I am *the survivor* of Kanda. The one in the papers?" I called Jones by his surname. No one else did that. He gave me permission.

"Wait, *the survivor*? The one who saw the Thieves of Otemachi?" Jones' eyes went wide, "I thought you were just in the area, not the actual guy who saw the Thieves."

"Are you sure you're a detective?" Hamada called from behind the curtain.

"Shut up, reporter. The real detectives are talking over here." There was the CDI Jones rudeness I knew and loved.

"I'm just saying. Zach Tragic is the modern day Kintaro. How do you have someone as famous as Kintaro living in your town and not know he is *the survivor* of Kanda?" Hamada threw back the curtain and stared at CDI Jones.

Her face was bandaged, but for the most part, she looked fine.

"Look lady, I only care about actual crimes. Stories and legends are not actual crimes. Talk to me about the Sumida killer or the extortion gangs in Hachioji. But the Thieves of Otemachi? The survivor of Kanda? Those aren't crimes so much as urban legends. Fairy tales you tell your kids to make them behave and avoid going out alone." Jones shook his head. He didn't believe the stories about Kanda. I was there. I knew better.

"So what about the head?" Hamada asked, challenging Jones.

"I'm done. You two want to talk about Kanda, fine. You don't need me." I stood and walked out.

"Tragic, wait. I need your statement." Jones said, "Look what you did, lady."

"What I did? Seriously, for a detective, you're really not very observant." Hamada replied to the detective.

I left as the two of them argued. I wanted to know why someone tried to shoot up my office. I didn't need to talk to a reporter and a detective about Kanda. And I was definitely not about to talk to those two about *him*. About his head. Not in this lifetime.

"Wait up." Hamada called from behind me as I walked back towards my office.

"I'm going home. Leave me alone." I called back.

"Where? To your office? I don't think the police will let you back in. It's a crime scene now. Probably the biggest crime scene in the entire city with the explosion and all the gunfire." Hamada caught up to me, but I kept walking.

"You have any other suggestions?" I asked facetiously. Hamada said nothing.

"I thought as much. Look, Hamada-san, you want a

story. Go find one. Somewhere else. You got blown up and shot at today because someone wants to kill me. A sensible person would get away before they get hurt." I tried to sound reasonable. People listen when you sound reasonable.

"I don't think they were after you." Hamada said. I didn't expect that.

"What do you mean?" I turned left as we crossed the street. My office might be a mess, but the coffee shop was still available.

"You're not the first person I asked about Kanda. I've been after this story for a while, and I think the attack might have been directed at me. I'm sorry. I might have brought my trouble to your door." Hamada looked like she believed what she was saying.

"So you want my story, you trashed my office, and you almost got both of us killed to get it? Don't you think you're giving yourself too much credit?" I asked as we reached the cafe door. I stepped inside and held the door for Hamada to follow.

"Oh, and someone wants to kill you ten years after Kanda? Ten years where you were so anonymous that most people forgot you didn't die? Who's claiming too much credit now, Zach Lejeune?" Hamada said as she smiled at me and tried to turn on the charm.

It's not that Hamada wasn't attractive or engaging, it's that I just don't care about things like that. I did care about getting some tea. Tea is better than attempts at manipulation.

"Sit. Have a tea or a coffee." I said, gesturing to the camera for a green tea. Hamada made a gesture I didn't recognize. We didn't speak until after the waiter brought my tea and a tapioca bubble tea for the reporter.

"Tell me why you think the shooter was after you, Hamada-san?" I sipped at my tea.

"I asked a lot of questions. Not everyone was happy about it. I also found this in my apartment." Hamada took a card out of her purse and placed it in front of me, then she picked up her bubble tea and gestured to the camera for a straw. I read the card.

"Well, that's vague. No threat. No topic. Just 'stop asking.' Seems reasonable that explosive arson and assassination would be the next step." I picked up the card. It was handwritten, but the characters were deliberately blocky. 'Stop asking.' The ink was dark. Not a ball point. The paper was heavy and smooth. This was an expensive note to send.

"It isn't the first time." Hamada said. She took the offered straw from the waiter and dropped it in her drink. Hamada drank through the straw, sucking up big orbs of tapioca that went pop as she pulled them up through the tube.

"The first time someone shot at you? Or the first time you received a vague threat?" I asked.

"The threat. Last time I investigated Kanda and the Thieves of Otemachi, I backed off when I got threatened. I was just a graduate student, and I scared easily." Hamada said as she put her drink down.

"Yet you still became a reporter. I would reconsider your career choice."

"No. I was studying folklore. I became a reporter later. You don't make a good living as a folklorist."

"So that's why you were asking about him?" I asked.

"About him? The head of Taira no Masakado? Are you on speaking terms with a 1,100-year-old corpse?" Hamada asked rhetorically.

"No. We are not on speaking terms." I said.

"Ha. Are you serious? I was kidding. You don't actually believe in kami, do you?" Hamada didn't expect a candid answer.

I sipped at my tea.

"All of it leads back to the Thieves of Otemachi and Kanda. You are the only survivor and so it all leads back to you. I think whoever wants to kill me also wants to keep whatever you know a secret." Hamada had rehearsed her speech. She kept going, trying to keep me from thinking through the implications of her words.

"So you must have seen something worth killing for when you confronted the thieves. Maybe you were in on it, maybe you saw something you shouldn't have? Maybe you don't even know what you saw? That's what I want to know, and that's why someone is trying to silence me. To stop me from talking to you."

"How long?" I asked.

"Since grad school." Hamada said.

"No. How long did you practice that speech? It was impressive, but you seem to have missed the most important point. If someone wanted you dead, they could have taken care of you before I ever got to my office. It isn't you they want dead. It's me." I let that sink in. Hamada was focused on her story, but she didn't know everything, "You're right about one thing. This is all about the Thieves of Otemachi, Kanda, and Taira no Masakado's stolen head."

"So what happened at Kanda? Tell me and maybe we can figure it out together?" Hamada was still after her story.

"No. I've had enough of gods and revolutionaries. I don't need that kind of hassle." I said. I didn't care about Taira no Masakado anymore. I through being famous.

"You sure about that, Mr. Lejeune? If someone is out to

kill you because of what happened at Kanda, why would they stop now?" she asked.

"I can handle it. I don't want anyone to end up dead." I said. I wasn't lying.

"You think your talent will get you out of it?" Hamada said, "The bad luck of Zach Tragic?"

"It helps, but I've been doing this for a long time. Experience counts more than other people's ill fortune." I was sure the conversation was going in the wrong direction. I didn't need to feel the bad luck in the air to know that.

"Whatever is going on, it's tied to Kanda. To Taira no Masakado. He revolted against the government in Kyoto, nearly overthrew the throne. His spirit lived beyond the grave and brought misfortune to those who offended him. Sounds a lot like you, Mr. Zach Tragic." Hamada finished her bubble tea.

"I can assure you, Hamada-san, I'm not Taira no Masakado. He is very dead and the last I saw, his head was in a box. The Thieves of Otemachi were buried at Kanda and the head with them." I said. The sense of wrongness increased. Something was going wrong, eagerly wrong.

"Then come and help me prove it. Kanda is restored. The remains of Taira no Masakado weren't found. Help me find him and restore his head to the grave at Otemachi." Hamada set her trap.

"No. I am done with Kanda." Saying it made me feel better.

"I'll pay you. Hire you to help me find the head?" Trap sprung.

"And if the shooter comes for you? Then what?" I asked.

"I'll hide behind you. Surely the hero of Skytree and the survivor of Kanda can keep me safe?" Hamada smiled.

"Will you leave me alone if I take you to Kanda? Go away for good and not bother me again?" I asked.

"Help me find the head and I'll do whatever you like."

"Fine. But I am not helping to find the head. I'm just taking you to Kanda. I'll show you where it happened and answer your questions. If the head is there, you can return it to Otemachi. But after that, leave me alone and stay out of my business?" I made my offer.

"Deal." Hamada answered.

"Wait until you see my invoice."

I finished my tea in silence, paid the bill for us both, and headed to the door. Hamada followed, and we made our way to the newly restored Kanda metro station.

We walked most of the way. The metro ran on a very limited schedule and we missed the Ginza line to Kanda. Before the Drift, the metro ran every few minutes. Now, out of an abundance of caution and general scarcity of power, trains ran every few hours.

Kanda Eki had been a small station on the Ginza line, the Japan Rail station above ground was far larger but because of the above-ground rail and the central location of the Ginza line itself, Kanda had always busy. The North Gate was closest to the Japan Rail station, and that was where I was ten years earlier.

"Is this where they found you, Zach?" Hamada said. I wasn't sure when on our journey she had started calling me by my given name instead of 'Mr. Lejeune.'

"Yes. The subsidence collapsed most of the above-ground rail station. The Chuo landed over there by Exit 3." I said, pointing across the newly restored subway track. We had entered through the number 4 Exit on the opposite side of the rails from Exit 3.

"The Chuo?" Hamada asked. She must not have seen the photos.

"Yes. The entire train came through the ceiling, just missing my head. The others waiting for the Ginza weren't so lucky." I said.

"Oh." Hamada was crinkling her eyes and face, trying to imagine a train in the space we now occupied.

"I had just come from the far end of the line, by the number 6 Exit. I ran into the Thieves halfway down the ramp." I said, walking quickly towards where I remembered bumping into the three brutish men and one tall, strikingly fox-like woman. I could feel the excitement returning to me as I approached the spot where we had met.

"Then what happened? The reports say you knocked the head away from them." Hamada was catching my excitement, or maybe she was always like this and I hadn't noticed it before.

"I didn't really do anything. I was late for an audition. The four of them were coming from the above-ground rail. I ran into them and they lost their grip on the box they were carrying. It fell down onto the tracks. The biggest man jumped after it without thinking." I pointed to the rails. Pillars lined the length of the tracks in between the northbound and southbound lines.

"So how did you know it was Taira no Masakado's relic?" Hamada asked as she stared at the pillars. The thick supports were mostly new construction, but two or three appeared to be original to the station.

"The woman jumped down to help and part of the box, maybe the lid, swung down. I saw the head. It was still covered in flesh, as if he was still alive. I didn't know it was *his* head." I pointed to one of the original pillars, "They stood right there. I recognize the kanji. It still says 'access way.'"

"The final report on the rescue efforts said they only recovered three bodies in this area." Hamada pulled a map out from her purse and inspected it. She showed me the markings. It was the report from the recovery teams that had done the initial operation to rescue any survivors. There was one circle by the North Gate. Dozens of x-marks represented the dead.

"There were four. And the head." I said.

"What happened next?" she asked.

"I ran to the station manager. I thought they had a fresh body. I thought they were yakuza. That's when I heard him." I said.

"What are you saying?" Hamada asked.

"Nothing. The bodies. Who did they find?"

"Three men. They were crushed and couldn't be identified." Hamada showed me the text that accompanied the map.

"She couldn't have gotten far. Where was the closest female victim? That's where the box should have been." I said, searching the map.

"What about there?" Hamada said, pointing to the tracks. I looked up. Access way. Of course. An escape route.

I jumped down on the tracks. The trains would not run here for another couple hours, so there was no danger. Circling the pillar, I found it, a steel access door on the far side of the pillar. It was rusty and probably didn't open.

"Well, all this time." I said as I turned the handle and tried the door. It opened easily. Hamada jumped down and walked up beside me. A ladder inside the hollow pillar reached down into the earth. It was rusted like the door, but it seemed solid. I tested it with my foot and it held.

"Me first." Hamada said and started down the old metal rungs.

"That's not how this works. You hired me. I don't get paid if you die." I said, climbing after the reporter.

The ladder ended in a tunnel that ran perpendicular to the rails. Every few meters a light gave off enough illumination to see, but not much more. Dust covered the floor.

"I don't think this was part of the renovation."

"You're right," I said, "Follow me."

We walked for a short distance and the tunnel ended. Set into the wall was a metal door, and debris covered the floor. I bent to examine it.

"Try the door, Hamada." I said.

"Why? What's behind it?" she asked.

"I don't know, but this is it." I said.

"What? What is that garbage?"

"That garbage, my dear reporter, is your story. It's the box that held the head of Taira no Masakado."

THE AMBUSH, THE HEIST, AND THE GRAVE

Climbing up the corroded ladder back to the tracks was a simple task. Getting out of the station was less simple. I didn't know it, but it might have been better to stay with the locked door.

"Watch your step when you come out," I said to Hamada, "It seems a little slippery."

"Give me a hand?"

I grasped Hamada's hand and steadied her as she transitioned from the access way to the rail tunnel. The sound of the rifle shot was deafening in the enclosed space.

"Time to pay the price, Tragic." The shout came from the direction of the North Gate.

I pushed Hamada back against the pillar and covered her with my body. She couldn't pay me if she was dead.

"Who are you? What do you want?" I yelled back. I heard the bolt on the rifle retract and then slam back into the receiver. Bolt-action rifle.

"Doesn't matter, Tragic. Today is the day you die." It was a man, but there was nothing else remarkable about his voice.

"I'm a bit busy. Could you come back some other time? Maybe never?" I tried to lean out and see where the shooter was standing. My reward was another loud crack as a bullet struck the pillar we hid behind. He knew where we were hiding. Maybe he saw me lean out, but I couldn't be sure. If he could see me, I could see him as long as I knew where to look. I kept looking until I heard the shooter retract the bolt to reload the rifle. I couldn't find him, but I ducked back just in case his line of sight was better than mine.

"When I say run, go to the next pillar." I gestured towards the opposite exit, away from the North Gate. Hamada shook her head in agreement. She was scared. Another crack rang out, and a bullet struck the pillar. I said the words.

"Run. Now." I didn't look to make sure Hamada ran. I jumped out away from the pillar and scanned the North Gate. I didn't stop moving. Jump back, then to the side, back again, and then I saw him. The rifle was down and his gloved hand was on the bolt. He was an amateur. I jumped to the pillar and ran after Hamada. I judged the angle that would hide me from the shooter best and stuck to my line.

I heard the bolt racking, another cartridge slamming home into the barrel of the rifle. Everything felt off. I made my move and leaped straight ahead, tackling Hamada to the ground. She was slowly running in heels. At least the shoes were wide, flat heels and not fashionable, ridiculous heels that would trip her up. She did well despite the one shoe having been roughly repaired with tape since the morning.

Another shot rang out. It went wide and I couldn't see where it might have hit. Again, the shooter didn't reload right away. A professional wouldn't wait. A professional also wouldn't lower the weapon and lose his sight picture on his target. Every moment he took to reload, look, and sight the weapon was another moment we had to evade and live. Hamada and I took this moment to scramble behind the next pillar.

"I'm coming for you, Zach Tragic. Time to meet your end." I heard the bolt locking. The action was jammed. I'd have bet money that the shooter didn't clean his rifle as often as he should. My talent was working. The carbon buildup in the barrel was likely fouling the action of the bolt as the shooter struggled to chamber another cartridge.

"Hamada, run." I said. She ran, and I followed. I could hear the shooter curse behind us. He slapped at the bolt, trying to free it.

"Where?" Hamada cried.

"There. Up the ladder." I pointed to the end of the passenger ramp where a short ladder ran down to the rail bed.

I heard the distinct sound of brass ringing out as the spent cartridge cleared the rifle. The shooter had freed the blockage. We were out of time. Hamada scampered up the ladder as I turned to look behind us. I had a clear line of sight on the shooter and he could see me. We locked eyes, and I tried to memorize his face. Jet black hair, cut sideways and stylish a few years back. Pretend military style, but edgy like a cavity. Staring, unblinking gaze. Great. Mil-fashion poseur.

The bolt slammed forward, and he raised the rifle to sight down on me. The moment the rifle lined up, I moved. I launched myself to the side, away from the ladder and towards the center of the rail bed. The shot ran out and hit the ladder. Amateur.

"What an idiot." Hamada swore, "Get up here before he reloads."

I ran, climbed up the short ladder, and pushed Hamada

in front of me towards the number 6 Exit. We ran up the stairs, taking two or three steps at a time. I could just hear the shooter struggling with the bolt again. I hoped he never learned to clean his gear properly.

"Head north. Get to the big road. Head towards Ogawa-machi. We can lose him in the crowds." I said, and Hamada ran. We turned left and followed the big road past Sudacho. We kept going past the entrances to Ogawamachi Eki.

"Where now?" Hamada asked.

I pointed. It felt wrong to my left. Bad luck for others would be good luck for me. I pointed towards the bad luck I felt. We headed south. I felt drawn towards the bad fortune. It was a familiar, yet distant feeling. I had felt this before. In Kanda ten years ago. Hamada and I were running towards Kanda bridge. I suddenly knew where we were going. Damn him. I slowed our pace as we reached the bridge.

"I guess you were right. He was after you, Zach." Hamada said.

"Forgive me for not feeling good about being right." I looked around, scanning the faces in the crowd for the shooter.

Tokyo may be Forgotten, but it's still one of the largest cities in the world. People were everywhere. I looked for the stylish black haircut. The piercing eyes. The giant damned firearm.

"What is this all about, Zach? He was shooting at us. I could have been dead. I think you owe me an explanation." Hamada crossed her arms in front of her and stared me down. She could be assertive when she wanted to be.

"I have no idea. However, if I were to make a guess, I would say he wants the head. Or wants it to stay hidden." I said.

"You think he was waiting for us? Did he know the box was there?" Hamada asked.

"I didn't know it was there. I think he would have been better positioned if he knew it was down that access way." I said, "But he's an amateur. He didn't understand how to do his job right. We would have been defenseless in that tunnel."

"How could you tell? I thought he was shooting like a pro." Hamada continued her line of questioning. That was one reason I was not fond of reporters.

"You know I was an actor before the Drift." Hamada nodded.

"I had a role in a net-drama. I realistic military thriller." I said.

"Wasn't that *Kudo's Repose*?" Hamada asked. She was right. She had done some of her homework.

"Yeah. That's the one. The director insisted that I train with a former special operations soldier from the Self-Defense Forces. She took pity on the poor actor and taught me everything she could." I might have smiled slightly.

"She?" Hamada made a lewd face at me.

"It wasn't like that. I'm not like that."

"Oh, really? A hot, young actor like you were? How old were you? Twenty? Twenty-two?" Hamada smiled. She didn't know me at all, despite her research.

"Whatever. I am not here for your lascivious imagination." I turned and started walking across the Kanda bridge.

"Hey, come on. I was just having some fun. Someone just tried to murder us both. Give me a break, ok, Zach?" Hamada followed me as we walked towards Otemachi.

"A pro would have waited for us at the ladder. A pro wouldn't have dropped his sight picture every time he took a shot. Most of all, a pro wouldn't have announced himself and talked like a villain in a spy thriller." I kept walking. We passed the post office and turned right. Our destination was around the corner.

"So what is this all about?" Hamada asked again, "I think you know and I want to know before your amateur gets lucky."

"I think it is about the Thieves of Otemachi and the head of Taira no Masakado." I said.

"Is that why we are going to his grave?" Hamada asked.

"Not really. He wants me here." I said.

"He? Who wants you here? The amateur?"

"Taira no Masakado."

"You're kidding me. Taira no Masakado has been dead for over 1,100 years. He's a decapitated head, for goodness sakes." Hamada laughed at me.

"A head that still has its flesh and looks like it died yesterday. Taira no Masakado is a kami. A very annoying and angry kami." I turned and looked at the space between three buildings in the financial sector of Forgotten Tokyo.

"Grab a seat." I walked to the bench next to the road. The seats were new. Ten years ago, there were no benches at the grave. Hamada plunked down next to me.

"The Thieves of Otemachi stole the only known relic of an actual kami. They took it from that grave, right over there in broad daylight. No one knows how they did it. You can see the entire grave site from the road." I looked at my hands. My teeth were on edge this close to his place.

"I know the stories. You don't actually believe he was a kami. A spirit? Maybe even a god? All that is just superstition." Hamada said she studied folklore, but she didn't believe in the things she had studied.

"Of course he's a kami. A god? Maybe, but if so, he's a

very minor god indeed." I explained to her, "I don't have to believe it. I know it. He's in here."

"In your head?" Hamada pushed my finger aside. I was pointing to my head. A head within a head.

"Yes. I first heard Taira no Masakado when I crashed into the box. He said 'Thank you.' Then he said, 'Free me.' I dismissed it as an overactive imagination for years afterwards. But I knew. I always knew."

"That makes you sound crazy." Hamada didn't pull away, if anything, she leaned in closer.

"I know it sounds insane. It is insane. And yet, I'm Zach Tragic. I'm a literal corollary to Murphy's Law. You've studied my history, how else do you explain everything that has happened since the 3rd Great Kanto Earthquake?" I said.

"Bad luck follows you. It isn't out of the realm of possibility."

"You know some people think the earthquake happened because of the theft of Taira no Masakado's head?" I looked at Hamada, trying to see what she was thinking in her eyes.

"Do you believe that, Zach?" Hamada asked.

"No. It happened because I didn't free him. I ran. People died. It was his fault, but it was because of me." I waited for Hamada's response. I knew how it sounded. It took me a long time to accept the truth, but when I did, Taira no Masakado confirmed it for me. He rarely spoke, but he did when I figured out why he was mad. Taira no Masakado is an unforgiving bastard.

"That doesn't just sound crazy, that is crazy, Zach. And I know you aren't a madman." Hamada didn't believe. Fine. I could live with that if she could pay my fee. I leaned in.

"Are you sure of that, Hamada-san?"

"Yes." Hamada said, "But that leaves one unanswered question."

"What would that be?" I asked, genuinely interested in what her question might be.

"The Thieves stole the head. You thwarted them at Kanda. Three of the Thieves died in the 3rd Great Kanda Earthquake." Hamada sounded like she had rehearsed a speech.

"And so did half the city and surrounding region of Tokyo." I added.

"One thief survived. We found the box, but we didn't find the thief or the head. So where is it? Where is the head of Taira no Masakado?" Hamada sounded triumphant. She had been waiting to ask the question.

"Why don't we go ask him?" I said and stood up. I walked to the kubizuka. I passed the obelisk and the informational plaque. Hamada followed.

"But he isn't here. The head was stolen." Hamada protested.

"It was. But he is still in here." I said, pointing to my own head.

"No, Zach. You aren't the head of Taira no Masakado."

"No. But I have part of his kami. They used to call it kamigakari. Spirit possession. In my case, it is more of a sublet." I stood in front of the grave. It was a simple, but elegant kubizuka.

I clapped my hands twice and bowed my head. Taira no Masakado heard me.

"I stay away from this place." I said.

"Why is that, Zach?"

"His power is strong here. Like a haunting. Taira no Masakado was interred in this spot during the Heian period. Villagers buried his head here. The place was called

Shibasaki and eventually it became part of Edo. At some point, the village came to be called Otemachi and by then it was part of Tokyo. Taira no Masakado was here almost the entire time." I was explaining to Hamada as if she was a child. Her job was to learn.

"Didn't they move the head to Kanda Myoujin?" she asked.

"His spirit was moved to the Kanda shrine. The move appeased his ego, but when you fool with his kubizuka, when you fool with his grave, people die. Over a dozen civil servants paid the price in 1928 after the 1st Great Kanto Earthquake. They died because the Finance Ministry was moved to this place. The head likes its space."

"But that's all just a legend. Disease was rampant in the 20th century. It was a primitive time compared to now." Hamada refused to listen. I ignored her words.

"The heist was the worst offense you could imagine. No one actually knew Taira no Masakado's head was still in his kubizuka. No one would have believed it. Yet the Thieves of Otemachi knew. Two nights before that fateful day, the Thieves of Otemachi drove a gardener's truck up to the side of the road where that bench is now. They covered the entrance with a small scaffold and draped a blue cloth over it while they did their work. There were five of them at the time. The Thieves and the one remaining gardener. The woman had killed the rest of his staff. Shot them dead. While the gardener worked on the trees and plants, the three men worked on opening the grave. The woman supervised." I didn't so much explain as I let the tenant in my head do the explaining. After all, he had been there and I hadn't.

"How do you know that?" Hamada asked. I ignored her.

"They lifted the top slab of the kubizuka. The grave, my

grave was opened. The Thieves of Otemachi put me in a box. Common thieves dared to touch my relic. Had I found my body, I would have struck them down." Taira no Masakado was always searching for his strong, healthy body.

"Zach, you're scaring me." Hamada said. I didn't think she was scared.

"I was a prize to them. They left with my head in a box. The slab was replaced, but first they filled my grave. A gardener lies it in now. He was a true craftsman. I admire him." The ground quivered slightly like thunder.

"Zach, what is that? An earthquake?"

"Not exactly. I told you his power was strong here. I stay away because he likes to tell stories when he is strong. Boring, stupid stories. The things I could tell you about the Heian." I turned and looked at Hamada.

The earthquake grew louder and stronger. Taira no Masakado receded in my mind. He was making the unlikely happen. The stone slab of the kubizuka rumbled and split open. We were thrown to our knees by the powerful, local-ized earthquake.

"What the hell, Zach? What is going on?" Hamada screamed at me.

"You shouldn't have put him up to it, Hamada. You gave yourself away. I figured it out at the station." I said.

"What are you talking about, Zach?" Hamada protested.

"The shooter was an idiot. You hired him to get me here. To find the head. Did you think I knew where it was? That I hid it all those years ago?" I asked. It all became clear when she called the shooter an idiot. It was her slip. She had hired an amateur and it showed. That made her mad.

Hamada had hired the best ten years ago when they stole the head. This time she had hired a moron.

I grabbed Hamada by the shoulder and forced her to look in the grave. The kubizuka was split open. Inside, the corpse of an elderly gardener lay as fresh as the day she had shot him ten years ago.

THE COLLECTOR, THE CONSEQUENCES, AND TAIRA NO MASAKADO

"Is that who you think I am? Some common thief? Zach, I thought you knew better?"

"No, you're not a common thief. You're a very rare, very special sort of thief. The kind that kills."

"If that's true, you should be very careful what you say to me, Zach."

"That's what I can't figure out. We remember you, but you looked very different ten years ago. You were pretty, like a fox is pretty. All angles and grace. You're still pretty, but now you're more round. Like ko-omote." I said, looking Hamada up and down, trying to see the vicious killer Taira no Masakado remembered.

"Maybe I look different because I am different. Did you and your kamigakari spirit ever consider that? And now that I think about it, isn't kamigakari for miko when they divine the future? You don't look much like a shrine maiden to me, Zach Tragic." she said as she looked me up and down while avoiding looking at the gardener's body.

"Yeah, I read about that after Taira no Masakado first started talking to me. Seems the legends aren't always right." I said. I couldn't tell if she was the killer or not. She didn't feel right. Something was ever so slightly off about Hamada Yu. Then I saw it, the glint of metal. Maybe there was more going on than either I or Hamada knew.

"Tell me, where did you get those scars, Hamada-san?" I asked.

"It's not any of your business, but given everything that happened today, I'll tell you. I was trapped under a fallen wall during the 3rd Great Kanto Earthquake." she said.

"I see the scars on your arms. I think I can see some on your neck. When did you start studying folklore?" I asked.

"After I recovered from the quake. I did something with my life. So I went to school." Hamada was getting annoyed at my questions. I couldn't blame her, I had just accused her of being a thief and a cold-blooded murderer. Not to mention the supernatural earthquake. I'm surprised she wasn't petrified with fear.

"Do you remember what you did before the earthquake?" I asked.

Hamada looked away.

"Ah, so there it is." I said.

"No. Alright? No, I don't know what I did before. I woke up in the hospital and that was it. When the wall fell, I caught it with my face. I was a blank slate. Traumatic injury induced amnesia." Hamada spat the words out like sour pickles.

"You don't even know who you are, do you?"

"No." I thought tears might have been in her eyes, but then again, perhaps not.

"I guess it doesn't really matter, does it?" I asked, not expecting an answer.

But Hamada didn't have time to reply. We both heard the crack of the rifle shot. I had no idea where the bullet struck as we both threw ourselves to the ground. I turned my head and looked Hamada in the face.

"Guess your amateur shooter found us?"

"Why does he have to be mine?" Hamada asked.

"Zach Tragic? Come home to daddy? Is it time to die, yet?" The shooter half-yelled, half-sang at us.

"Why would you hire such an idiot?" I asked Hamada.

"I didn't hire him or anyone. I'm a reporter. Your Taira no Masakado has it wrong." I could feel Hamada's breath on my face.

We were so close that I could see the thin lines, the ito of natto scars running across Hamada's forehead and back to the base of her neck. Her hair was thrown back and away from her face. I saw the glint of dull metal and a socketed port on the knobby bone of her skull. It was an old stabilizer of some sort. The type of personality stabilizer used to treat head traumas like she said she'd suffered during the 3rd Great Kanto Earthquake. No wonder.

"Look, we have to move or even this wanna-be killer is going to become the real deal." I said as I tried to see over Hamada and out into the street.

"Come out, Zach. Bring your pretty girlfriend and I'll give you both a nice grave." The shooter was hanging back. He really was an amateur. Surprise had been on his side. He could have set up a clear shot and taken us both out before we knew what had happened. Instead, he shot wildly and shouted with bravado. Too many movies and manga. Professionals get the job done and move on.

"You know we're trapped? Three walls and only one way in. Unless you count the kubizuka?" Hamada was thinking out loud.

"Don't count it. No one is coming out of there alive." I said, knowing it was true. Knowing it.

"Hamada, when I tell you, run to the far corner. Head for that old tree. Hide. I have a plan, or at least the beginning of a plan." I said.

"Great. And then we can settle this thing about me being a killer if we aren't both dead." Hamada agreed.

"Deal. Now move on three. One. Two. Move!" I jumped up and ran the opposite direction from Hamada. She made it to the tree, and I didn't hear a shot. The shooter hadn't learned. The bolt opened and closed as I hid behind a large rock, closer to the entrance. I waited for a shot. Damn it. The amateur didn't commit to a wild shot. Now this would be harder.

I scraped my fingers across the ground. Pebbles and enough dirt for my needs. I waited.

"I saw you run, Tragic. Running like a scared little squirrel. I'm coming for you." The shooter yelled. I looked at the kubizuka and the spot where Hamada and I had dropped to the ground. It might have been a guess, because he said nothing about Hamada. Maybe he didn't see her run. And that meant he was on the far side of the entrance, away from me. If he came directly in, I didn't stand a chance.

Hamada knew I had been an actor. You learn things about lines of sight and positioning on a stage when you're an actor. We call it blocking. If the shooter saw only me, he had to have his view of Hamada interrupted by something. A tree, a rock, the obelisk. The side of the building. Were that true, he was directly ahead of me with the building on his left side. I was on the far right side of the entrance to the gravesite. A big rock with a memorial bronze plaque was on my side of the entrance. I was hiding behind it. If the shooter entered the site, he could just stay to his left, cheating right and he would have me dead to rights. Probably where the English phrase came from, shooters on the right side of a gunman are more vulnerable unless the shooter is left handed. A left-handed gunman has to cross over his own body to shoot someone on his right. A right-handed gunman has the full arc of his right side available for killing. I think about that sort of thing when people are trying to murder me.

Lucky for me, the shooter was a moron. He must have been afraid of missing, because he kept walking towards the memorial plaque and didn't enter the grave site. I could hear his footsteps on the other site of my hiding spot. No doubt he was planning to jump out at me and shoot. He must have thought if he was point blank that he couldn't miss. Amateurs. I backed around to the far side of the rock. There was a low, metal tube fence that ran along the front of the sidewalk. The fence ran right up to the side of the rock I was backed up against. I put my foot on the metal tube and gently boosted myself up, clinging to the rock.

As I expected, the shooter jumped out, trying to surprise me where I had been hiding. He shot without waiting to see if I was actually there. Rifles are loud at close range and very intimidating. I had been around rifles and pistols enough in my acting career that I didn't get intimidated by their report. I pushed off the fence and out over the rock. My other foot hit the rock as I threw the pebbles and dirt into the amateur shooter's face. I pushed off again, using the rock to push myself up and over the shooter. It wasn't a graceful arc, but it didn't matter. My aim had been true. The shooter screamed and dropped the rifle. His eyes were peeled wide in sick anticipation of shooting me in the face, or gut, or whatever. Perfect for my pebble and dirt surprise. He clawed at his face, trying to get the grit out of his eyes. It must have stung.

I tucked and rolled, coming up easily on my feet. I look like a scarecrow. All bones and cruel angles, but I was still graceful. Being an actor for net-dramas in Japan required a certain level of gymnastic ability, and I tried to keep in shape. I turned to face the moron while still crouched.

The rifle was right there in front of me, so I snatched it up by the barrel and swung it towards the shooter as I rose to my full height. A little extra momentum couldn't hurt.

The rifle butt struck him full in the chest and knocked the air from his lungs. The shooter staggered back, coughed, and stumbled into the kubizuka. The open kubizuka. He fell backwards into the open grave.

I felt sick. This wasn't how things should end. Taira no Masakado was pleased, and that made me feel even sicker. I knew the amateur shooter, the wanna-be assassin, was dead. I didn't need to look. I could feel it and it felt terrible.

"Zach? Are you alright?" Hamada spoke from behind the tree.

"Yeah. As much as I can be alright." I gripped the rifle stock and brought the action up to my face. I released the magazine and safed the weapon. More acting experience. Who would have guessed faking it on a stage would come in so handy when people were trying to kill you?

"We need to call the police." Hamada peeked out from behind the tree.

"You can come out. It's safe. The police will be here soon enough." I said as I walked over to the kubizuka. The shooter lay on top of the gardener. I tossed the rifle down to its dead owner. I kept the magazine.

"Zach! Is that a good idea?" Hamada asked, walking up to the grave one slow step at a time. She peered down at the two dead bodies. She covered her mouth with her hand and gasped. Maybe she had never seen a dead body before today? Hamada ran her hand through her hair, holding her scalp like a person in distress.

"It's fine. Nothing comes out of that grave alive." I said.

"Well, I guess that is one way to settle a score? What do you think, Lejeune-san?" she said. I didn't need my talent to feel the wrongness of the situation.

"Ah, so there it is. You're not Hamada-san anymore, are you?" I asked, not looking at the reporter.

"How did you know?" she asked.

"I saw the stabilizer when we were on the ground. You said a wall fell on you. I can just make out all the scaring on your face. You had a lot of plastic surgery. The stabilizer must have been to help with the trauma. I bet it's an old model, isn't it?" I was piecing together the evidence as I spoke.

"Yes. The first personality stabilizers were fine for a short time. Unfortunately, they don't always hold up over a couple years. Mine didn't last 9 months." she said.

"Personality fracture? You had a psychotic split?" I asked.

"Quite. The results of the surgery were shocking, but I saw that as an opportunity. No one knew me anymore. It was a chance I couldn't resist." The reporter walked around the kubizuka.

"I stashed the head and tried to get out when Kanda fell. I got trapped under a wall, but I was far enough away that no one connected me to the station or the theft. I decided to make a fresh start and collect the head after everything settled down." The reporter looked at the bodies. The expression on her face was completely different from when she was Hamada Yu.

"So what do I call you?" I asked. I was genuinely curious about my adversary.

"Inari will do for now." she said.

"A little presumptuous, don't you think?" I walked around the kubizuka. I tried to keep the grave between her and myself.

"And you? Claiming to have an 1,100 year old kami in your brain? I think we can both be a little presumptuous." Inari said.

"Yeah, well I guess my career took an unexpected turn somewhere along the line. Maybe about ten years ago. I think you might remember that day?" I tried to keep the emotion out of my voice. I failed.

"My career died that day, too. You don't know how much money and suffering you caused me, Mr. Lejeune." Inari, the woman I had known for so short a time as Hamada Yu continued to walk around the open grave.

"Oh really? And what career was that? Thief? Murderer? Gang leader?" I needed to draw the conversation out. The police would be here soon enough. Gunshots just don't happen in Forgotten Tokyo. Once the police from the local koban were authorized to draw weapons heavier than their revolvers, they would be here in no time at all.

"I was a retrieval expert. An art dealer for a very select clientèle. You interrupted the repatriation of Taira no Masakado's relic. My client was not pleased. Of course, neither was I. What with this new face and an infernal personality stabilizer. Who would be?" Inari was angry, but her anger was focused and seething. She was not one to make mistakes.

"Shame. Maybe you'll get time off for your suffering when they convict you?" I chided Inari. I thought I could goad her into being rash. It was the best I could hope for at the moment.

"Oh, I don't think so. I'm innocent. Hamada Yu has no

idea she's just an overlay on my true persona. I made sure to whisper cautions into her dreams. Be careful. Don't do anything to attract attention. Find the man who did this to us. Eventually she found you. Took her long enough. I guess that is what happens when you're just an overlay on the brilliant original." Inari believed every word she said.

"I still don't understand. You had a chance at a new life, why go back to trying to steal the head? Why go after me?" I slipped the magazine into my vest pocket. I wanted both hands free if she made a move.

"A new life? I was split in two. Half of me was that blundering girl, Hamada Yu and her obsession with folk-lore. Me, the real me, was trapped. I managed to manifest when she was stressed or deep asleep, but that isn't living." Inari's eyes glimmered with something more than anger.

"I set up that fool, Ando-san to try and take you out. I knew he was an idiot. Just a military wanna-be with a rifle and an attitude. I need to get the head back and trying for years to get Hamada to do the work? Infuriating." Inari seemed to like talking. The personality stabilizer must have done a good job of scrambling her brain.

"Naruhodo." I said.

"Don't you get cheeky with me, Lejeune-sama." I didn't like the way she said -sama.

"Naruhodo." I doubled down.

Inari let out a scream as she leaped across the kubizuka. It surprised me. She lost control so quickly, probably a side effect of the malfunctioning stabilizer. Inari hit me full in the chest and we both went down. I rolled and tried to keep her from tearing at my face with one of her hands. The nails were sharp and she scratched me up a bit more than I liked.

"Get off!" I yelled.

"Oh? I thought you might like this? Aren't I pretty

enough for you? Don't you have a smart word or two for me, Lejeune-sama? I thought you liked tough women, judging from your landlady?" Inari stopped scratching as she sat on top of me with my leg bent up between my chest and hers. Instead she started punching me in the face. She was good at it. I began to feel not just pain but also the rising unease of my talent manifesting.

"Not interested. I don't care about things like that." I said, trying to get my hand up to block Inari's punches.

"Naruhodo." Inari said, mocking me.

"Fine. Just stop hitting me." I said as I caught her fist in my hand and restrained it.

"Well, I do care about it. You're not the pretty bishi-boy you were ten years ago, but that hardly matters." Inari said as she leaned in and planted a grasping kiss right on my mouth. It was more than I could take.

"Get off." I said as I bunched up the muscles in my lower back and pushed the weight of Inari off with my legs. She staggered as she stood and stumbled back. I felt my talent swell and I heard the snap. The crudely repaired heel on Inari's shoe broke and she tumbled back, falling into the open grave.

I stood up and spat. I never spit.

Looking down, I saw Inari fumbling with the rifle.

"Won't do you any good." I said as I touched my vest pocket. It was empty, the magazine was gone.

Inari smiled as she slapped the magazine home in the rifle's receiver. The earth began to tremble. Inari looked around in a panic.

Taira no Masakado was a nasty, petty kami. The entire site of the tomb rocked as a sudden earthquake shook us and knocked me off my feet. The slabs that had covered the kubizuka rocked and moved. The one on the right slipped and fell down, into the grave. I looked away. If revenge was what this was about, Inari brought a weak hand to play against Taira no Masakado on his home ground.

I stood up and turned to walk away. I was done with this.

"If you're alive in there, Inari or Hamada-san, or whoever you really are, say hello to the cops for me." I walked away as I heard Inari pounding on the slab, trying to beat her way out to freedom. No one comes out of there alive, or at least in one piece. Inari went into there in at least two pieces. I wasn't sure I wanted her to come out.

"You're a real bastard, Taira no Masakado, you know that, right?" I said to no one in particular.

"I am, aren't I, Zakurai?" No one in particular said back to me.

A REQUEST FROM M&W BOOKS AND M. DAVID SCOBLE

I hope you enjoyed reading *Zach Tragic in Forgotten Tokyo*! Leaving a review at your preferred book seller is a great way to help me, and any author out! Every positive review helps to bring our books to the attention of other potential readers. Please consider helping us out by leaving a review!

AFTERWORD

Would you like to get more short stories for free? Join the *M&W Books Pack*! We send a newsletter with a free short story every month!

Click *M&W Books* to join the newsletter or scan the QR code below!

ACKNOWLEDGMENTS

Zach Tragic would never have happened with my father.

My first experiences learning about living in a city were with my father. I learned to be at home, to be comfortable in a city. There were three periods in my life where the relationship with my father has grown. As a child, I saw him on television and visited, but did not understand. As a teenager, I began to learn who he was. I looked forward to the summers I spent with him in the big city. Finally, as an adult, I have tried to make sense of life. I have failed at that as miserably as any of us. What I have learned however is that I have never said "thank you" and "I love you" enough.

Zach Tragic is part of saying that some more.

ABOUT THE AUTHOR

M. David Scoble

M. David writes from a secluded location in the heart of Tokyo. Surrounded by a variety of inconvenient Yokai, Yurei, and a pair of very lazy hounds, M. David happily devotes modest amounts of free time to exploring the worlds of supernatural creatures, high science, and the cybernatural world to come.

Moogi & Wil Books
www.mandwbooks.com

instagram.com/zachinoate

pinterest.com/pinaccount0360

goodreads.com/mdavidscoble

amazon.com/author/mdavidscoble

ALSO BY M. DAVID SCOBLE

The Generators Sequence

The Generators Sequence

The prison ship should have been dead when the final failsafe, Tristan 08 awoke. But Xander, the Evolved leopard spy had no intention of dying that day. That chance meeting would throw two civilizations into conflict across the stars...

...this was just the beginning...

Four short stories from the M&W Books Newsletter - *The Generators Sequence*, by M. David Scoble - available now!